Death Masque

A Sebastian McCabe—Jeff Cody Mystery

Dan Andriacco

First edition published in 2018
© Copyright 2018
Dan Andriacco

Paperback ISBN 978-1-78705-313-7
ePub ISBN 978-1-78705-314-4
PDF ISBN 978-1-78705-315-1

Published in the UK by MX Publishing
335 Princess Park Manor, Royal Drive,
London, N11 3GX
www.mxpublishing.com
Cover design by Brian Belanger

This book is dedicated to

Deacon Ken Ramsey, Sr.

soldier, lawman, cleric, and McCabeophile

CONTENTS

ACT ONE

ACT ONE

Chapter One
A Big Fish

The first mystery about Hunter Davenport was why my boss, the redoubtable Lesley Saylor-Mackie, summoned me to a meeting with him on that Monday morning in mid-April. I'd never met the man, although I'd heard his name bandied about town plenty.

"Oh, yes, the PR guy," he said when Saylor-Mackie had pronounced our names to each other. "Good to meet you, Jeff."

My wince was partly from hearing my position as communications director at St. Benignus University dismissed so blithely, and partly from a handshake that indicated Davenport had put in serious gym time. I never trust a man with a grip that disables me from picking up a pen afterward.

Davenport was a hard-charging businessman who had golden-parachuted into Erin after being pushed off the top of the Amalgamated Brands corporate ladder in Chicago. What had brought him to small-town Ohio was his wife, Erin-native Nadine Lattimore. The former beauty queen had longed to return to her hometown after a stint as an Emmy-winning TV reporter in the Windy City. Now she was an anchor in Cincinnati, forty miles downriver from her new home just outside of Erin and making a far less stressful daily commute than she'd faced in Illinois.

Her somewhat-older husband, his age somewhere north of fifty, had meanwhile reinvented himself in Erin as a developer. His inaugural project was a proposed boutique (as in "expensive") hotel about which everyone in town seemed to have an opinion, most definitely including Sebastian McCabe. Mac had dragged me into this controversy as well, despite my initial indifference. I'd heard that the former Fortune 500 honcho was determined to become a big fish in a small pond. Mac had strongly suggested that the fish in question was a shark. And I don't think he meant "shark" as in entrepreneurs who invest in promising businesses. He never watches that show.

"Please sit down," Saylor-Mackie invited both of us. She moved out from behind the aircraft carrier-sized desk dominating her office, a legacy of her predecessor, and occupied a stuffed chair herself.

Just short of my six-one, Davenport had a full head of suspiciously dark brown hair and steely eyes magnified by rimless glasses—eyes that missed nothing. He looked impressive even sitting beneath a painting of President Taft. The portrait of the great Ohioan had come with Saylor-Mackie when she'd inherited the large office at the beginning of the academic year as our new executive vice president and provost. This followed a long and successful stint as head of SBU's history department and almost two terms as mayor of Erin.

A historian with an extraordinary talent for administration, she'd authored an award-winning biography of Taft's later life called *William Howard Taft: Mr. Chief Justice.* And she looked the part of the accomplished administrator—a perennially elegant woman with never a formerly-sandy gray hair out of place. My awe of her had only grown in the short time I'd been reporting to her. Never mind that parade of racy romance novels she'd written under a pseudonym. Everybody needs a hobby.

"I'm sorry to pull you in on such short notice, Jeff," she said, "but it's a surprise to me, too. Mr. Davenport is here to discuss a major contribution to the popular culture program."

So that was why I'd been invited to this party! Since becoming my supervisor, Saylor-Mackie had been gently encouraging me to be more proactive in pushing out the good news. Or, as she put it, speaking more as a football fan and former politician than as an academic, "It's time to play offense." With that as the game plan, my brain immediately started crafting a press release without any instructions from me: *St. Benignus University, a four-year Catholic liberal arts institution, is pleased to announce a generous donation of . . .*

"Fifty thousand dollars, to be exact," Davenport said, grabbing control of the conversation.

I would have raised an eyebrow, Mac-like, but I've never mastered the trick. The popular culture program at St. Benignus *is* Sebastian McCabe. He teaches most of the courses and hires adjunct instructors and guest lecturers for the rest. It's a very small program and much despised by our former provost, the recently departed Ralph Pendergast. So why would Hunter Davenport, of Davenport Development, be donating money to the nemesis of his pet project? That's one reason for the eyebrow I would have raised. The other is that, while an amount like that would get lost in the rounding for a large state or private university, it was big enough for SBU that our president normally would have been involved in the handover.

"Father Pirelli asked me to meet with Mr. Davenport," explained Saylor-Mackie, who apparently had already worked with me long enough to read my mind.

If we'd been alone I would have observed to her that Fr. Pirelli, who had passed normal retirement age during the Clinton Administration, had been looking tired lately. He'd confided to me that he wanted to step down from his essentially figurehead position, but he thought that SBU had already undergone too much change lately with Ralph's departure. Saylor-Mackie, upon taking over the number two spot in the university hierarchy, had managed to get "executive vice president" added to the front of her job title to reflect the power of her position.

I pulled out a notebook to make a few scribblings. "I don't recall seeing your name on our donor lists, Hunter." *If I'm "Jeff," you can be "Hunter."* What's euphemistically called "development" or "advancement" in non-profit circles isn't part of my job at the university, but I've always figured it doesn't hurt to know where the money comes from. So, I pay attention to the names of our biggest backers. There aren't so many that it's a chore.

"No, this is my first contribution to St. Benignus." Davenport sat forward a bit, looking very earnest. "I've been supporting other civic causes since I came to Erin— St. Hildegarde Health, the local opera, the art museum, and so forth. But I've long been a reader of Sebastian McCabe's mystery novels."

Another surprise. "I wouldn't have taken you for a Damon Devlin fan," I said, keeping it light.

"Who?"

I gave Saylor-Mackie what I hoped was a meaningful look, the meaning being, *"What game is he playing?"* That annoying magician-sleuth Devlin is the hero of every one of Mac's twenty-six implausible books, including the latest, *The Devil and Damon Devlin.* Although Mac's greatest creation is and always will be Sebastian McCabe, any real McCabe reader would know the name of his protagonist. Ergo (as Mac might say), Davenport was having us on.

"Of course," the faux fan added without waiting for me to answer his question, "I would expect that with added funding for his department Professor McCabe would be quite busy and no longer have time to spend on extra-curricular activities."

Saylor-Mackie sat back as if she'd been slapped, although her face remained an emotionless mask. "Extra-curricular activities such as?"

She knew where Davenport was headed with this, but she wanted him to say it.

"I don't mean to imply that he would or should stop writing books." *Heavens no!* "But he should stick to that and leave the civic activism to somebody else. He's made a fool of himself by opposing my plan to redevelop the Bijou Theatre site. That 'Save the Bijou' nonsense of his is standing in the way of progress. If we greatly expand the existing bike trail along the Ohio, and add my new hotel, Erin could capitalize on the river to pull in regional tourists from Ohio, Kentucky, Indiana, and even West Virginia. They would spend a few days and more than a few dollars in this town, which is why the Convention & Visitors Bureau supports my plan."

He was in full salesman mode. Heck, I could just imagine myself breezing along the river on my Schwinn. But Saylor-Mackie wasn't buying.

"Your plan to tear down the Bijou building has been rather controversial," the Provost understated. In fact, it had been the biggest local controversy since the St. Patrick's Day parade the year before.[1] The populace of Erin was sharply divided between preservationists, led by Mac, and those who favored development the Davenport way. With city elections seven months off, candidates for mayor and City Council had firmly staked out their positions—as had the denizens of all our bars and beauty shops.

"Professor McCabe's position is not the position of St. Benignus University because we don't have one," my favorite historian continued. "We try to be a good corporate citizen, but that doesn't require the university to take a stance on every public issue. It also doesn't mean preventing a tenured professor—or even a first-year instructor—from actively engaging in the public square, as is her or his civic right. In fact, we encourage it. Saving the

---

[1] See *Erin Go Bloody*, MX Publishing, 2016.

venerable Bijou Theatre seems to be quite important to Professor McCabe, and I'm sure that he will find time to continue fighting that battle even if he should be so fortunate as to acquire enhanced responsibilities with the popular culture department."

In other words, Davenport, take your clumsy bribe and stick it in your ear or other bodily orifice!

"You might want to rethink that, Mayor."

She shook her head. "I'm not the mayor anymore, and I'd prefer to not use the honorific." She'd given up the side job when she moved up the SBU ladder, although she wasn't required to. That move had answered my long-pondered question of whether her political or her academic ambitions were greater—at least for the time being. She still wore business suits during daylight hours.

Davenport tried again.

"Suppose McCabe—"

"I learned a long time ago never to engage in hypotheticals, Mr. Davenport, especially when they involve Sebastian McCabe. I grant you that even on a university campus freedom of speech is not absolute. However, in the real world—the one in which we do not have to suppose—Professor McCabe has said and done nothing inappropriate to his position, no matter how much you might disagree with his opinions or his rather vigorous actions."

"Then I guess we can't do business, Madame Provost."

"Not under your implied conditions, we can't. I'm sorry, Mr. Davenport. The strings you want to attach are untenable to me. Thank you for your visit." *And don't let the door hit your ass on the way out.*

The developer stood up. "I happen to know several members of your board of trustees and I don't think they'll be happy when they find out you turned down a significant donation out of a misguided sense of rectitude."

Saylor-Mackie allowed herself a Mona Lisa smile. "Oh, I suspect that I know my trustees better than you do."

"We'll see about that."

With a couple of curt nods, Davenport cut his losses and left.

"He didn't say goodbye," I complained.

"That was clearly a man who isn't used to being turned down. No doubt we haven't heard the last of him. But I'm not worried. One thing this job has in common with being mayor is that it's important to know how to count votes. I know that some trustees will be unhappy, either because of the immediate loss of the contribution or because they don't want to get crosswise with Davenport. But there won't be enough of them to cause us any real trouble." *"Us."* I liked that. "How do you think Ralph would have handled this situation?"

As head of the Sussex County Convention & Visitors Bureau, the former provost was all onboard with Davenport's plan to build the Bijou Hotel. But as provost—

"He wouldn't have kowtowed. Five years ago, he might have, but he grew in the job. I think if he were still behind that desk he would have pushed back just as strongly as you did, even though he hated the whole idea of the popular culture department. Ralph's shorts are more than a little too tight, but he has what Davenport might call a sense of rectitude."

"I agree. Ralph didn't leave me any surprises to clean up." She hates surprises, so I try not to give her any. "Gulliver warned me about Davenport." Her long-time spouse, Gulliver Mackie, is an investment advisor who also invests in real estate, which once caused a bit of a problem.[2] "He also suggested that if the Bijou redevelopment project doesn't go through, the old theater would be an excellent opportunity for St. Benignus to have a presence downtown.

---

[2] See *Bookmarked for Murder* (MX Publishing, 2015)

That appeals to me. I've been thinking about the desirability of a footprint in the heart of the city for some time."

"Gown meets town," I quipped. "Actually, Mac has already talked to Kendric Armstrong about that possibility." Kendric is the head of BSU's theater department.

"I'm not surprised. Mac's crusade doesn't seem to have missed a bet. I presume you've had a behind-the-scenes hand in that, Jeff?"

"You could say so."

Chapter Two
"I Need Your Help"

"Jefferson, I need your help."

That's where it had started for me, with a conversation in Mac's man cave—he calls it a study—at the beginning of April. The calendar said spring but the wood fire at Casa McCabe delivered a welcome warmth to my chilled bones. Mac's words, however, were not so warming. Everybody wants to feel needed, but Sebastian McCabe calling out the reserves could not be a good thing.

Mac, who is married to my sister Kate and is my best friend other than my wife, usually draws on his own vast reserves of ability and energy to get things accomplished. After all, he is a magician among his other talents. So, I regarded his immense bulk and bearded visage with a certain apprehension that evening. And rightly so. By the time this mess was over, I'd be involved in political corruption, two murders, and a night at the opera—though I couldn't really blame Mac for the opera.

"What now?" I demanded.

The big guy poured himself a locally brewed beer from the tap. "Are you fami by a man named Hunter Davenport to tear down the Bijou Theatre and build a boutique hotel on the site? And this with the proposed assistance of tax incentives from the city of Erin?"

"I've heard something to that effect. And good riddance to the old building, I say. I think it's been vacant for at least as long as I've lived in Erin. It's an eyesore. And Front Street is prime real estate!" In fact, the abandoned building was flanked by two bustling businesses. The Sweet Shoppe candy emporium sat on one side, as it had for decades. A Touch of Glass, a high-end gift store where you might be offered a mimosa in the morning if you hit the owner in the right mood, flanked the other side.

"An eyesore?" Mac boomed, arching an eyebrow. "Only for those with no vision, old boy! The rich history of the Bijou should stir the imagination of anyone with a pulse. Why, the very name recalls the era when big cities and small towns alike had great theaters with names like Lyric, Capitol, Palace, Majestic—and, yes, Bijou. Our Bijou was built in 1881 as a vaudeville house. Professor Carlo Stuarti, the immortal 'Count of Conjuring,' performed there before it was converted into a silent movie house in the 1920s. So did Harry Blackstone Sr., Benjamin Sterling, and a veritable *Who's Who* of other prestidigitators. I believe it quite likely that the stage still retains trap doors."

"Fascinating," I lied.

"Therefore, I believe it has great potential to be resurrected as a theater for live performances."

"We already have one of those, remember?"

The question was purely rhetorical. Of course he remembered! Mac himself had written and starred in *1895,* the first play performed at the Lyceum Theater. And that had required Mac to swallow a healthy helping of pride. For the dynamo behind the successful project to renovate a former vacant Odd Fellows Hall into a theater was Mac's old frenemy, Lafcadio Figg.

A shared interest in mysteries and Sherlock Holmes had brought Mac and Figg together even before the latter moved to Erin. But the sparks thrown off by two enlarged egos rubbing against each other whenever they interfaced made their relationship a rocky one. Figg was currently indebted to Mac for solving a murder in a way that caused the least embarrassment to the former drama teacher,[3] although I wasn't sure Figg understood that.

"Admittedly, Jefferson, some of our fellow citizens take the small-minded approach that one legitimate theater is enough for a community our size," Mac rejoined. "I regret to say that Lafcadio is among them. He is not in our corner."

"*Our* corner?"

"Exactly, old boy! I knew you would see the light! And who but you, with your well-honed expertise in shaping public opinion, could best help me convince the Historic Conservation Board and the Zoning Board of Appeals to block the demolition of the Bijou? We are about to become civic activists!"

"Speak for yourself. You can take a position on anything you want, as long as it isn't politically incorrect, and nobody will care. You're a full professor, therefore both job-secure and expected to be squirrely. Nobody would assume that you speak for the university. But with me it's different. I *do* speak for the university. That's part of my job description, a big part."

"Your role in the battle to save the Bijou would not be widely known, of course."

"All work and no glory, as usual!"

Mac's hirsute face assumed an air of injured innocence, as if he couldn't imagine what I meant.

"Still, the challenge of planning a campaign to stop the bulldozers does have its attraction," I mused, intrigued despite myself. "A small number of people on the two boards and City Council will make the key decisions, and they are all politicians or people appointed by politicians. Now, it's a well-kept secret that trying to change people's minds is almost a complete waste of time. Once human beings have decided what they think, they're too invested in

---

[3] See *Queen City Corpse* (MX Publishing, 2017).

being right to let the facts stand in their way. And most of the time facts have nothing to do with what they think anyway. But in this case, we don't care if the key decision-makers change their minds, we just want them to vote our way. Who's for us and who's against us at this point?" *Did I say "our way" and "us"?*

"Harriet Ballou, of the Historical Society, wants to preserve the building whether it can be resurrected or not, naturally."

"Naturally."

"So does the Erin Preservation Society."

"I've never heard of the Erin Preservation Society."

"Neither has anyone else, I assure you. It is a somnolent organization. I am about to become its most active member.

"On the other side of the issue, our old bête noir Ralph Pendergast supports the hotel project as a spur to local economic development. That is to be expected from the Convention & Visitors Bureau, and therefore discounted. Hunter Davenport already has financing for his project lined up through Gamble Bank, so your old chess partner is also firmly in his camp." I had once played the sport of kings with Amy Quong, executive vice president of Erin's home-grown bank, during a brief period when we were both in residence at the same B&B. She beat me in six moves, which Mac will never let me forget. "City Council at this point appears evenly divided on the matter, four to four, if I read the tea leaves correctly. It could become an issue in the election, even for the mayor."

"The mayor doesn't vote on Council matters."

"He does when there is a tie vote. He also has veto power over action items."

Reverend Fred Sutterlee, formerly president pro tempore of Erin City Council and vice mayor, had moved up to acting mayor upon Lesley Saylor-Mackie's resignation. But he wasn't a candidate in the three-ring circus that was the race for a full term as mayor, opting instead to run again for Council. His replacement on Council, Leonidis Garrison of the eponymous antiques store on Main Street, was a placeholder without political ambitions.

"What about Serena Mason?"

The richest—and most generous—woman in Erin would be on anybody's dream team to support a civic project.

"There are rumors that she's been asked to finance a plan to renovate and repurpose the Bijou, which is laudable but premature. First, we must prevent its demolition. If we can accomplish that, then I suspect that Davenport's Plan B would be to sell the building at a handsome profit. There must be at least one potential buyer waiting in the wings, if the tittle-tattle about Serena is true."

Wheels turned in the Cody brain.

"We need to consolidate existing opposition to Davenport, add to it, and mobilize," I said. *Hey, that's not bad!*

"Mobilize in what way?"

"Well, we need to get some A-list Erinites, prominent citizens, to testify before the preservation and zoning boards. But we should also get their names and a lot more on an ad in the *Observer*. That will catch the attention of the politicos."

"Ah, yes. 'The press, Watson, is a most valuable institution, if only you know how to use it.'"

When Mac quotes Sherlock Holmes, I ignore him. "The idea is to show mass support. We don't want to make this seem like an elitist cause for the wine and brie set." *Even though it kind of is.*

"What would you suggest in addition to an advertisement?"

"Take a multi-front approach to show big numbers on the preservation side of the debate. Just off the top of my head, we could picket City Hall, start an online petition, distribute yard signs all around the city, and launch a social media campaign with a Facebook page and a *#savethebijou* hashtag."

This was my wheelhouse and I knew what to do, though I seldom get to go full bore like this as communications director for SBU.

Mac smiled. "Well, then, old boy. Game on!"

If this was a game, it was chess – a lot of strategy and it's not over in a hurry. Unfortunately, I'm not a great chess player. (See Amy Quong.) If I were, maybe I would have paid more attention to the player on the other side well before that day I met him in Lesley Saylor-Mackie's office.

Chapter Three
Taking Names

In a movie, you would now see a montage of the Bijou campaign coming to pass just as I'd envisioned on the fly—the yard signs, the online petition, the social media stuff.

It took a couple of weeks to really crank it up, but the operation launched just a few days after our man-cave confab. Mac and I went calling on some of Erin's leading residents to get them on board first. I was careful in each case to point out that I wasn't representing St. Benignus University, or its faculty, staff, students, or mascots. Our mission was to collect signatures for a newspaper ad that said **SAVE THE BIJOU** at the top in 72-point type. After an overwritten (by Sebastian McCabe) history of the building, the ad ended with what they call in development circles "the ask":

> *As concerned citizens who realize that we cannot secure the future of Erin by forgetting its past, we urge the Historic Conservation Board and the Zoning Board of Appeals to block the proposed demolition of the historic Bijou Theatre. If these boards fail the community, we ask that Erin City Council overrule them by city ordinance and, further, that Council deny the owner's request for tax incentives to build an unneeded hotel on the site.*

The official sponsor of the ad was the Erin Preservation Society, largely a fig leaf for Mac. I think it had about five members before he joined and dominated it.

Serena Mason, an energetic septuagenarian with short salt-and-pepper hair and wide hazel eyes, signed the letter almost before Mac finished asking. She also autographed a check with a small (for her) contribution to the budding Save the Bijou crusade. We hadn't even thought of begging for money, but she insisted. "You know I love old buildings," she commented with an expressive look around our environs. "I'm just sorry I don't have the time or the uncommitted funds to make a bigger contribution at this point."

We had met with her at an old mansion that now houses some of the programs of Serenity House, Erin's premiere social service agency. The organization is one of the prime beneficiaries of the Mason Foundation, the vehicle through which Serena cheerfully redistributes her late husband's family money as well as her own. Not coincidentally, the landmark building is located on Front Street just a few blocks from the Bijou. Mac had decided to begin the search for signatures among the old theater's neighbors, figuring that would be a good barometer of whether more than a handful of citizens would share his passion to #savethebijou.

"Your support is quite important and much appreciated," Mac assured Serena. "And your testimony before the Historic Conservation Board will carry weight, given both the long Mason pedigree and your personal credibility. I gather from word about town that someone has approached you with an alternative plan for the Bijou site that would not involve destruction of the building. Are you willing to confirm or deny that?"

"My, tongues do wag, don't they?" Serena looked amused. "And sometimes they even know what they're talking about. It's true that someone did come to me for help on what seemed to be an exciting and promising project, Mac. Unfortunately, the best I could do was give advice. My time and money are largely committed here, and what's left over goes to four other boards I'm on."

Despite all the soft soap Mac had so diligently applied, Serena declined to cough up any details of the anonymous entrepreneur's dream for the Bijou restoration. "It's not my place to talk about it. The individual involved came to me in confidence."

The rest of Front Street was a mixed bag. Adam Mendenhall, director of the Shinkle Museum of Art, quickly signed on the dotted line. Clarice Stanfield, owner of the tony A Touch of Glass gift shop, offered up several high-minded reasons for supporting Davenport's plan to tear down the old theater building, including her assertion that it was an eyesore. "Only for those with no vision," I informed her. I was polite enough not to ask how many crystal decanters she expected to sell to guests of the projected new boutique hotel.

Wade Pennington, proprietor of the Sweet Shoppe on the other side of the Bijou, was blunter about his self-interest.

"Hell no, I'm not in favor of tearing down the theater," he said, grabbing Mac's ad to sign it. "That putz Davenport wants the city to take over my building by eminent domain to provide a bigger footprint for his damned hotel." Surrounded by Bit-O-Honeys and Tootsie Rolls, it was no surprise that his face was roughly the shape of a Moon Pie. But he wasn't heavy. His short-sleeved shirt hung loosely, as if he'd recently lost weight. He had thin, ginger hair that almost disappeared into his high forehead.

"What would I do if I got forced out of here? I've worked here since I was a boy helping my dad stock shelves." Those shelves went almost up to the ceiling, and were filled with glass jars of Bull's-eyes, Mary Janes, licorice . . . I could feel a cavity coming on just from eyeballing the stuff. "It's not as easy to relocate a store as you might think. It takes people a while to find you. You lose business." *And candy!*

"I sincerely hope you will not face that problem," Mac averred.

On our way out, I picked up three bags of licorice hats, one bag for Lynda and one for each of the unborn twins for whom she insisted she was eating. Later, at home, my grateful spouse did not let my thoughtfulness go unrewarded.

And so it went for the next few days as Mac and I continued signature hunting.

Henry Knox Wilcox, the pompous and opinionated freelance reviewer of all media for the *Erin Observer & News-Ledger*, offered moral support but said it would be unethical for him to sign the ad. Bobbie McGee, owner of the sports bar that bears her name, had no such concerns, and said she would write a "Save the Bijou" campaign song to boot.

We did not ignore the political class. The eight seats on City Council, for which a slew of candidates was competing in an at-large free-for-all election, potentially could have more sway over the fate of the Bijou than the mayor. But Mac reminded me that the mayoralty is a bully pulpit.

"'Unneeded hotel' is right," said mayor hopeful Reginald Fortesque III, echoing the words of the ad. "I've got a better idea: How about rezoning to allow container cars to be fixed up to provide cheap housing for the homeless?"

"Innovative," Mac judged.

"Damn right. And I'm going to make it happen when I'm mayor. It's part of my 12-point platform. You can see it on my website."

Fortesque, who had worked as a barber for most of his sixty-some years, had been homeless by choice when he first showed up in Erin.[4] Now he lived in a houseboat on the Ohio River, where we called on him. Trying to enjoy the millions he had won in the Ohio lottery, he no longer dressed his powerful physique in clothes that looked like something I had turned down at the St. Vincent de Paul store. He wore an ascot, a yacht captain hat, and a $300 pair of deck shoes. But his attitude, which had earned him the nickname of "Scrappy Smith" in his incognito days of homelessness, was as pugnacious as ever.

"I don't see my opponents' names on this ad," he observed. "Don't tell me those morons are in favor of this harebrained project to turn an unused theater into an unused hotel."

Hey—not a bad line! I made a mental note of it. The "unused to unused" part, I mean, not the name-calling.

"The positions of the others remain to be seen," Mac told Fortesque. "You are the first mayoral candidate we have approached."

"Oh. Well, you started in the right place. Good luck finding that pinko Alvarez."

"I believe she technically would be classed as a neo-Trotskyite."

Given that Lani Alvarez's millionaire grandfather in Florida had departed Cuba one dark night in a leaky boat sometime in the 1960s, I often wondered what the Alvarez family Thanksgiving dinners were like.

"We'll just look for a demonstration and find her under one of the picket sign," I quipped. "Or the only one." I was only half-joshing. Protesting was Alvarez's specialty, which is why we didn't *want* her name in the ad. She was too controversial, to the point where she might turn off some potential supporters of preservation if she lined up on our side.

---

[4] See "Art in the Blood" in *Rogues Gallery* (MX Publishing, 2014).

During her student days at St. Benignus—which seemed to last forever—Alvarez's Young Socialist Brigade had officially been decertified as a campus organization because of its atheist constitution. (Don't ask me why an atheist has Our Lady of Guadalupe tattooed on her right arm; I'm no theologian.) Last year she'd charged a campus police officer named Jackson with police brutality for allegedly "personhandling" her during a protest rally. The whole thing was a little muddy because Alvarez and Jackson had been romantically involved previously. Nevertheless, SBU's legal counsel, Kelly Richards, advised a settlement to get her out of our hair. I know we offered too much because she took the money and ran. I was just glad that she ran completely off campus and was no longer a student. And I sure as heck wasn't going to go looking for her!

Councilmember Bruce Gordon, the third candidate for mayor, was easy to run down in his floral shop on Mulberry Street, right next to the public library. The shop window was decorated with one of his campaign signs bearing the slogan "Vote the Rascal In" above a smiling picture of Gordy. Mac gave him the pitch and the wording of the ad for his signature. The old contrarian held the ad at arm's length, extending it out over a pot belly and a pair of suspenders decorated with images of edelweiss. He appeared to regard it with suspicion, although Mac had counted him as one of the four City Council members opposed to demolishing the Bijou.

"Looks like you've got all the important people in town signed on," he said, as if that were a fatal flaw. I've always thought that Gordy likes flowers a lot more than he likes people—not a great attribute in a politician.

"Not all the important people," Mac said suavely. "That is why we are asking you to add your name."

If Lynda had been there, she would have rolled her beautiful gold-flecked brown eyes. But Gordy ate up the honey Mac was pouring him, though he tried not to show it.

"You don't want them to demolish the old Bijou, eh? I have fond memories of that place. Back in high school, I used to sneak in there on Saturday afternoons. It was a dirty and smelly and showed the kind of movies . . ." He grabbed hold of himself, sparing us any more of his poignant reverie. "Well, anyway, I think you have the right idea, McCabe, trying to save it. Just because something's old, that doesn't mean it's bad. I'm old myself." He signed his name with a flourish. "Now, are you going to vote for me for mayor?"

Mac lifted an eyebrow. "Surely you do not intend to buy my vote with a quid pro quo, Councilman Gordon?"

Surely I do, Professor McCabe.

"No, of course not. That would be illegal." *Wink wink, nudge nudge.*

"I never did like that guy," I told Mac on the way out, making no special effort to keep my voice down. Nevertheless, I carried a box of two dozen long-stemmed roses with Lynda's name on it. You can't go wrong investing in flowers and candy for a pregnant wife.

"As a Councilman, he's a great florist," I added. "He's quite the artist with floral arrangements, and most of the town knows it. I bet the only reason he gets elected to Council over and over is name recognition." The highlight of Gordy's long City Council career had been defending the non-existent right of a technophobe to carry a banner in the St. Patrick's Day parade. That whole episode hadn't ended well, especially for the murder victim. "You don't really think he could become mayor, do you?"

"Have you considered the other alternatives facing the electorate, Jefferson?"

"I've tried not to. The lunatic vote for mayor is going to be split three ways."

We visited City Hall the next day in our quest for signatories to the ad, even though most Erin City Council members are seldom in the building except for meetings of

Council or various committees. I hadn't been to the Civil War era brick pile on Main Street very often myself since Saylor-Mackie had resigned as mayor. Not much had changed, though, including Allison Channing.

She looked up from her computer screen with a smile when she saw us approaching. "Well, look what the cat dragged in and forgot to eat! What brings you distinguished gentlemen into this den of iniquity?"

When Allison had first arrived at City Hall right out of high school, near the end of the Nixon Administration, she had been called a secretary and typed on a manual typewriter. Now one of two administrative assistants for City Council members, she must have been over seventy years old. But she dyed her hair, although I could never figure out the color, and she had the body of a runner.

"We're looking for an honest man or woman," I joked.

"You must need a new GPS."

During this badinage, Mac was admiring the poster in Allison's cubicle. And well he might—he was featured on it. Designed by Kate, it advertised a fund-raising event for the Lyceum Theater Corp. over the Fourth of July weekend a few months in the future. Under the theme of "A Night at the Music Hall," it was a Victorian-style variety show featuring "McCabe the Marvelous, Master of All Mysteries." And that was her toned-down version of his suggested moniker. Kate's artistic rendering of her husband had made him look mysterious indeed, emphasizing his dark eyebrows and Svengali eyes. Smaller images on the poster showed the Joyful Noise trio, a juggler, a plate-spinner, a unicyclist, and a thirteen-year-old ventriloquist—Mac and Kate's son Brian.

I cleared my throat, breaking Mac's concentration on himself so that he could join the party.

"We were hoping to add the names of some Council members to an advertisement seeking to preserve the Bijou Theatre from destruction," he explained to Allison.

"That's a good cause," she said. "I'm behind you all the way. I'd sign your ad myself, but it wouldn't be appropriate. Civil service and all."

"You are still a citizen, Ms. Channing, and this is a non-partisan effort."

"I like to keep my head down. That's why I'm still here. I've outlasted eight mayors so far."

"Speaking of which," I said, "is His Acting Honor in the house?"

"Yep. I'm sure he'd be happy to see you."

Reverend Sutterlee, a rotund black man brimming with equal parts enthusiasm and optimism, was in the mayor's office reading the Bible. I know how it ends, but I didn't want to spoil it for him. The reverend pastors the Apostolic Holiness Church of the Holy Spirit and, in his spare time, sings tenor with two other clergymen in the trio collectively known as Joyful Noise.

"The office suits you, Reverend," Mac commented.

The political pastor looked up with a reflective expression on his face. "Thank you, Professor. I appreciate that. I begin to think, gentlemen, that I made a mistake in not throwing my own hat into the ring for mayor. This campaign is a disgrace. Where is the cry for justice?"

"It's not too late to mount a write-in campaign," I pointed out.

"Perhaps not," he mused.

"More immediately," Mac rumbled, "we were hoping that you would lend your good name to a newspaper advertisement I have composed."

Within five minutes we had his signature. As a bonus, we snagged another one from Councilmember Chad Hollings on the way out of City Hall.

On the other hand, our venture into the arts community for support wasn't the no-brainer success that I'd expected it to be.

By the time we got to Jordan Webster, impresario (i.e., founder and artistic director) of the two-year-old Erin Opera Company, he was already preparing for the opera's next production at the Lyceum. *Claudette* would be the world premiere of a two-act opera about pirates in old New Orleans, with both libretto and music composed by Luther Kressel of the St. Benignus faculty. I once heard a vacuous talking head on network TV spout that "Leonardo da Vinci was a real Renaissance man," but the Mona Lisa maestro had nothing on Luther. With five master's degrees, Luther teaches history and economics at BSU. I'd already written a press release and tweeted about his opera.

In its first season, the Erin Opera Company had launched with *Amahl and the Night Visitors* (a big Christmas season hit) and *Pagliacci*. The second season had begun with *Markheim*, based on the Robert Louis Stevenson creeper. These were all short works, one or two acts as the company got its collective feet wet. *Claudette* was only slightly more ambitious, having just four main characters. But there were also two minor singing roles, a maid and an unrequited lover, plus lots of non-singing crowd parts for tone deaf people who wanted to be in the opera.

Jordan Webster, whom I'd never met before, looked remarkably ordinary as he stood on the empty stage of the Lyceum when we arrived there. Of medium height and slight build, with close-cropped dark hair and big round glasses, he wore a red turtleneck sweater over blue jeans. He was twenty-nine years old, with the eagerness and passion common to that age. And his passion, I soon learned, was not just opera but his opera company.

"I've heard a lot about you," he told Mac after our self-introductions. Only later did I realize that he may have been referring, in part, to a wife's-eye-view from Kate. An artist by vocation and a children's book illustrator by trade, my sister had volunteered to work on set designs for *Claudette*. Although the opera company was professional in the sense that paid performers came in from out of town to sing the lead roles, it was also a community venture made possible by a lot of volunteer time and effort.

"The experience is mutual," Mac said.

"Kate's designs are perfect, just what we needed."

"Doubtless," Mac said. "I eagerly await the production. Meanwhile, Jefferson and I were hoping you would sign an advertisement for the *Observer* supporting preservation of the Bijou Theatre."

Webster's cheerful demeanor went on vacation. He looked uncomfortable.

"That would be very difficult for me."

That rated a rare double-eyebrow lift from Mac. "Historic preservation is not the only issue here, Mr. Webster. The Bijou was once a great theater for intimate performances, and it could be again. The Erin Opera Company might fit in very well there."

Webster nodded gloomily. "I'm sure that's true. But I might as well be honest: Hunter Davenport, through his company, is the presenting sponsor for our entire season. And I'm hoping he will continue in that role next season as well."

The young impresario seemed reluctant to connect the dots, so I did it for him. "And since Davenport is the guy who wants to tear down the Bijou, you don't want to bite the hand that signs the checks by lining up against him."

"It would be rather ungracious of me, don't you think?" Webster at least had the grace to look sheepish.

"I concede the point, though I regret it," Mac said, with a slight bow of defeat.

"I'm sure my signature wouldn't make much difference to the powers that be anyway. Come back in May and enjoy the opera."

"You may be sure of that."

"I could have argued the power of numbers," I told Mac on our way out of the theater. "His signature might not mean much on its own, but it would as one of hundreds. A bundle of sticks is stronger than just one and all that. But Webster wasn't looking for a reason to sign, was he?"

"No, I sense that Mr. Webster is like an honest politician who, once bought, stays bought."

That humorous (if hackneyed) aphorism would come back to me later when an actual politician . . . well, you'll see.

Dante Peter O'Neill, recently given a newly-minted title as Dean of the School of Arts and Humanities at St. Benignus University, was eager to climb on Mac's bandwagon. Topping me by four inches at six-five, with a thin mustache barely visible against his dark skin and a penchant for three-piece suits, O'Neill's own background was in the fine arts. But his domain now included the drama department headed up by Kendric Armstrong.

"Be sure you see Kendric," O'Neill advised. "As long as the Bijou doesn't get torn down, there's hope that SBU might be able to acquire and restore it. Kendric would kill to have a venue like that in the heart of downtown."

Chapter Four
Campaigns and Controversy

Kendric Armstrong signed the advertisement, along with 113 other solid citizens. Toward the end of the signature-gathering process, it was like rolling a ball downhill. People we hadn't even thought of were contacting Mac to offer their John (or Joan) Hancocks to tack on.

Mac's op-ed piece, part of the campaign from the day I hatched it, appeared in the same edition of the paper under the stirring headline "Save the Bijou, Save Our History!" As a call to action, it wasn't bad, combining the emotional and the logical to great effect after Lynda and I tweaked Mac's first draft. A sampling here will give you the flavor of it. It began by framing the issue for those unaware:

> The Bijou Theatre, where once great magicians made their lovely assistants disappear, is now in danger of itself disappearing. A developer who bought the long-abandoned building proposes to demolish the structure and build a boutique hotel on the site. The Historic Conservation Board will take up the issue on May 3.
>
> This is no small issue. The Bijou in its day saw performances not only by great magicians but also by the Marx Brothers, Adele and Fred Astaire, W.C. Fields, the Andrews Sisters, and other legends too numerous to mention. It was an important part of Erin's

past, and could be a dynamic part of our city's future as well. When history is lost, it can never be regained. It is critical that the Historic Conservation Board not grant permission for the demolition of this cultural treasure.

After another nine paragraphs, the op-ed ended with an appeal to show up at the meeting of the Historic Conservation Board—a key but not definitive moment in the drama.

The one-two punch of the ad and the op-ed appeared in the *Observer & News-Ledger* on April 16. Hunter Davenport appeared in Lesley Saylor-Mackie's office on the morning of April 17 to proffer a donation with more strings attached than a marionette. A co-incidence? I think not!

"My word!" Mac said, upon learning of Davenport's ham-handed effort to shut him down. "He must view me as a substantial threat. That is excellent news indeed!"

"He's feeling the sting," I agreed.

The *Observer* ad and op-ed must have been only the proverbial straws that broke the developer's back. *Save the Bijou!* yard signs had popped up around the city like dandelions the week before, and the social media campaign was in full swing. Was it my fault that tweets on both sides were downright anti-social?

My twitter feed was filling up with stuff like:

Historic buildings make downtown Erin unique. #savethebijou

People before buildings: new hotel = new jobs. #bijoucango

Low-wage jobs suck. #savethebijou

Why is it better to be unemployed at $15 an hour than to have an honest job at less pay? #bijoucango

Because low-wage jobs suck AND it's not fair. #savethebijou

He bought it, he owns it, let him do with it whatever he wants. #bijoucango

Hunter Davenport is a rich carpetbagger who wants to get even richer off of Erin. #savethebijou

Twitter handles have been withheld to protect the guilty. And on it went, getting even worse after the op-ed and Davenport's retort in a similar space in the *Observer* two days later. But Mac, it should be noted, kept his tweets positive even as the Historic Conservation Board meeting neared. He bemoaned to me the behavior of those who didn't do likewise.

"Alas, Jefferson, the 'digital divide' is all too real. The term used to refer to the gap between those who embraced digital culture and those who did not or could not. Nowadays it might better describe the use of social media to seek reinforcement from likeminded digital 'friends' instead of employing Facebook, Twitter, and the like to engage those with whom we disagree. And thus, our culture slides ever further down the path of division instead of dialogue."

At least, I think that's what he said. Something like that, anyway. I only half-listened as a I tweeted out a link to a YouTube video of Bobbie McGee singing the song she had written for the campaign, "Theater of Love." It's a country-western ballad about a superannuated woman looking back at her lost youth and recalling happy memories of the Bijou Theatre. Said memories had nothing to do with what happened on the stage or screen, however. Either Bobbie's great-grandmother had lost her sense of discretion in her later years or Bobbie had made it all up. I didn't ask. It had a nice melody and a good pitch to save the Bijou.

Downloads of the music video and requests for yard signs surged after the op-ed and the ad, right along with the tweet storm. Sebastian McCabe probably couldn't have stopped the momentum at this point even if he'd wanted to, which he didn't. Somebody had even started a change.org petition, which I hadn't thought of. I've never known one of those to change anything, but I guess it couldn't hurt.

"I've had a few calls from unhappy trustees," Saylor-Mackie informed me toward the end of the week that she had shown Davenport the door. "Just the ones I expected, though."

"Pressuring you, are they?"

"Well, they're certainly giving it the old college try." She smiled as if she were enjoying the tussle, which she probably was. "It's nothing I can't handle."

The hearing before the Historic Conservation Board wasn't the only hurdle that the Bijou's noble defenders faced, but it was the first one. After that would come the Zoning Board of Appeals and maybe Erin City Council with the possibility of tax incentives for Davenport's hotel, to the delight of about sixteen non-incumbent candidates in search of an issue for their fall campaigns.

Nevertheless, I was buried in chores related to the upcoming edition of *Ben*, our university alumni magazine, when Mac popped his massive head into my office on the afternoon of May 3. My indispensable assistant, Aneliese "Popcorn" Pokorny, and I had been slaving over the issue for weeks. Now we were down to proofing the pages. To be specific, I was giving a close eye to the photos of traveling alums in exotic locations holding up the previous issue. You'd be surprised at some of the pictures that get sent in for that feature, and that's a surprise I didn't want Fr. Pirelli and our trustees (even the happy ones) to experience.

"Well, Jefferson, shall we go?"

It was Mac, of course, standing in front of my desk.

Only then did I remember the Conservation Board hearing. "Can I bring popcorn?"

"Would she be interested?"

"Never mind." I'd meant the snack suitable for munching during circuses, but a lame joke is never worth explaining. Leaving the communications office in Popcorn's more-than-capable hands, I headed with Mac over to City Hall.

An SRO crowd was already packed into the hearing room by the time we arrived at 1:30, a half-hour before the scheduled start. Encouragingly, many of the familiar faces belonged to folks who had signed our ad. I took some pride in that. I love it when a plan comes together, as Shakespeare or somebody said. Also, Johanna Rawls of the *Erin Observer & News-Ledger* was there to cover the story. She's a great young reporter, having learned everything she knows from Lynda, her first editor at the paper.

Promptly at the stroke of 2:00, Alicia Larkin, the attractive young black woman who chaired the commission, called the meeting to order. She sat at a kind of dais at the front of the room with the other six commissioners, four of whom were approximately twice her age.

"We don't have a big agenda today, but clearly there is a high-interest matter before us," she commented dryly. "That would be our first item, the application by Mr. Hunter Davenport, of the Davenport Development Co., for a certificate of appropriateness for demolition of the former Bijou Theatre building at 618 Front Street. Mr. Davenport, as the applicant, will have fifteen minutes to speak. Board members may ask questions. Then anyone else who has signed in today will be offered the opportunity to speak for up to two minutes. Mr. Davenport may then cross-examine such speakers, also for up to two minutes. When everyone else has had a chance to speak, Mr. Davenport has the right to a five-minute rebuttal. I hope that is all clear."

Ms. Larkin ran a tight ship!

Davenport, decked out in a gray pinstriped suit and a navy-blue tie, looked bored in a "Do I really have to put up with this chicken outfit?" kind of way. But he gamely put a smile on his maturely handsome face as he stood to speak.

I wondered where he got his hair dyed, and how much it cost him.

"I love Erin." Davenport looked around at his fellow citizens, oozing concern and sincerity. Not all the looks back at him were hostile. Despite the success of our adventure in civic activism, the town was still of two minds about what some saw as a clash between preservation and progress. "I wasn't born here like many of you, but my wife was. And when Nadine said she wanted to move back here, I understood why." That was a nice touch, I thought— mentioning the hometown beauty queen and TV anchor. "It's a charming place to live. Part of that charm is its history as an old river town that was a major stop on the Underground Railroad. I wouldn't change that for anything.

"But there's something I *would* change, my friends. The failure to capitalize on our natural advantages has stalled our recovery from the Great Recession. That's why I invested, along with a partner, in a new bike and canoe rental business on Water Street. And that's why I bought a decaying old building several blocks away for the site on which to build a new boutique hotel for visitors. Just imagine the economic ripple effect if we could entice the visiting parents of college kids to stay a few extra days in Erin because there was something for them to do and a nice place to stay."

Or imagine those SBU kids skipping classes in favor of a canoe jaunt down the Ohio.

Davenport went on a bit while I checked e-mail on my phone.

"My economic feasibility study has convinced me that a hotel at that location, of the size and nature I plan, is viable," he was saying when I tuned back in.

"I've already had preliminary architectural drawings drawn for the hotel. Those of you who know anything about such matters will realize that I've already spent a lot of money on the project, in addition to the cost of buying the building. Frankly, pulling the plug now would create an economic hardship for me." *Cue the violins!* He would have been better off leaving out the bid for sympathy, IMHO. Davenport wouldn't exactly be hitting up passersby on Front Street for spare change if his project went south, and everybody there knew it. "So, I respectfully ask the Historic Conservation Board for a certificate of appropriateness for demolition of the long-abandoned Bijou building so that the property can be made available for its highest and best use."

One of the board members, an older specimen with big ears, hopped right on the developer's closing pitch. A plate identified him as Elmo Dowd. I strongly suspected that he was a retired accountant or engineer.

"Why isn't restoring the building—either to its original use as a theater or for some creative repurposing— the highest and best use of the property?" he asked. "Why didn't you opt for preservation over destruction?" The man could turn a phrase.

"That may sound good, but it isn't economically viable based on the condition of the building, Mr. Dowd," Davenport retorted. "It would cost millions just to make it safe, without even considering the question of making it usable. I ran the numbers on that as part of my feasibility study."

"But that study was based on certain assumptions, wasn't it?"

Translation: You rigged it to get the outcome you wanted, didn't you?

"Of course. Any such study has to be based on some assumptions about human behavior."

Translation: Yes, I did.

"It seems to me that you're asking this board, in part, to act out of sympathy for the economic position that you put yourself in," Ms. Larkin said. "After all, the Bijou building was in its current state when you bought it eight months ago."

Davenport allowed himself a sheepish grin. "I must concede that I am not an experienced developer."

"That's not our problem," Dowd observed.

The inexperienced developer kept the grin, but I could tell he wanted to slug the old guy.

"I'm concerned that we may lose something of architectural significance if we let you demolish the Bijou," said a heavy, gray-haired board member named Charles Curtis.

"My architects tell me that the theater is indistinguishable from others of that era," Davenport fired back. "Apparently the country is still full of them."

"But Erin isn't, sir."

I wish I'd brought that popcorn.

That wrapped up the inquisition from the board. Not all onlookers took advantage of their shot at two minutes of fame, but enough did to keep it interesting. Ms. Larkin reminded them to step up to the microphone, identify themselves for the record, and spell their names. The first to do so was Ralph Pendergast, my former boss and now head honcho of the Visitors Bureau.

"The Sussex County Convention & Visitors Bureau enthusiastically supports Mr. Davenport's vision for a livelier riverfront," he said. "For too long we have underutilized this resource. A hotel on Front Street would go a long way toward addressing that deficiency. We believe that it will bring in new visitors from around the region, not take away from our two existing hotels and the many fine bed-and-breakfasts."

To be fair to Ralph—which is a new policy for me—I don't see how the president of the Convention & Visitors Bureau could take any other stance. I kind of wished he hadn't mentioned the B&B's, though, since Lynda and I had almost been murdered in one of them just before our wedding.

Several other witnesses came forward on both sides. Kendric Armstrong, a tall specimen with a gray mustache and pony tail, made it clear that he didn't represent St. Benignus University when he spoke against the demolition. But he also noted that his drama department needed a new theater and downtown Erin would be a great location for it. Serena Mason opined that old buildings should be saved, not demolished. She also argued that an expensive new hotel near Serenity House—which provides showers for the homeless, among other services—wouldn't be a good fit.

But Lafcadio Figg, a stout old soul who affected side whiskers that General Burnside would envy, gamely tried to make a case that others couldn't do what he and his group did with the Lyceum: rehab and repurpose a big old theater. "Our support was strong and the availability of money for social enterprises was much different then," he alleged. *Yes, it's better now.*

Wade Pennington, the candy man with the Moon Pie face, blistered Davenport and the horse he rode in on. Mac and I had heard that song from him already, and the lyrics hadn't changed for a bigger audience. But he ended with a nice closer:

"It's true that Erin doesn't have a new hotel. It's also true that we don't have a Chicago or New York City crime rate. Should we try to get that, too? One of the things we do have is a damned good candy store. My family has been selling candy to your family at the Sweet Shoppe for four generations. Now Davenport's complete plan, which he failed to mention today, includes having the city take over our building by eminent domain for his project because I won't sell out to him. Sure, I could move the store to a new location, but it just wouldn't be the same."

That earned Pennington applause, though not from Davenport.

Next up was Bruce Gordon—from candy to flowers. Mac cocked an eyebrow, and I could guess what he was thinking. Gordy had signed the ad, but we'd never expected him to man the barricades for the cause.

And how right we were!

"This is a farce," he began, tugging on his floral-themed suspenders. "A man should have the right to do whatever he wants with his own property. Davenport here bought the building. He should be able to tear it down, paint it pink, or have an inflatable gorilla climbing up the side." *The Bijou isn't tall enough for King Kong, Gordy. But maybe the hotel will be.* "This is America, after all—life, liberty, and the pursuit of happiness. And when I'm mayor . . ."

He went on like that for another minute and twelve seconds before Ms. Larkin cut off his mic.

Elmo Dowd leaned forward. "Let me get this straight, Mr. Gordon." He held up the two-week-old *Observer* ad which I hadn't noticed on the table in front of him. "Your name is one of more than a hundred on this advertisement asking this body not to issue the certificate permitting demolition of the Bijou Theatre. Isn't that true?"

"I guess you could say that."

"I'd have to say it. It's true!" Mild chuckles rippled through the room. "Now you're arguing for just the opposite. What gives, Gordy?"

I found out later that Dowd and Gordon had been classmates together at Malcolm C. Cotton High School in the late 1950s and early 1960s. They were generally on good terms—up to then, anyway.

"What's this country coming to when a man can't change his mind, Elm?" the political florist retorted. "Besides, I was pressured into signing that stupid ad."

Sebastian McCabe was rendered speechless by this exchange, an unprecedented occurrence which was worth the price of admission all by itself. If vaudeville had been this good, the Bijou never would have gone out of business.

Entertainment value aside, Bruce Gordon's defection was a double blow to our cause. City Council was now on Davenport's side, five to three, instead of evenly divided. And if he became mayor in November, he could use his veto power over action items to cause no end of mischief as the issue dragged on in its various aspects.

"Tall Rawls should check into whose filling up Gordy's campaign war chest," I told Mac after the hearing adjourned. Johanna is a six-footer without her high heels, and she is seldom without her high heels. "He didn't change his mind for no reason."

"In this case, old boy, I suspect that your usual cynicism is not misplaced."

"Mr. McCabe?"

We turned around. To my surprise, the interrupter was Jordan Webster, our local opera impresario. I'd noticed him in the audience, watching with great interest behind his large glasses, but he hadn't come up to the microphone. Mac greeted him cheerfully despite his refusal to sign the "Save the Bijou" ad.

"I was wondering whether I could have one of your yard signs," Webster said.

Mac arched an eyebrow. "We have a few left and I would be delighted to share one with you. May I ask why your change of mind on the issue?"

"Ms. Larkin and Mr. Pennington—their observations were very persuasive."

"Well, you're a little late to the party," I observed. "Today was the big day."

Chapter Five
The Long Wait

But the Historic Conservation Board didn't announce its vote for more than a week, which seemed much longer while we were waiting it out.

Meanwhile, the *Observer & News-Ledger* kept finding ways to keep the story alive with new angles. They included a historical piece on Erin theaters that no longer existed, an interview with the candy man, and a look at Paddles & Wheels, the bike and canoe rental operation on Water Street that Hunter Davenport owned with a 22-year-old business partner named Sheila Paxton.

"Good work," Lynda opined as she showed me the latter over breakfast on the Saturday morning after the hearing. "This Paxton woman seems like a real go-getter, and quite accomplished for her age. I'm kind of surprised that Davenport would partner with anybody, the way you described him."

"Women-owned businesses have an edge in minority set-aside programs," I reminded her. "Maybe he was working that angle."

My favorite journalist, known as Lynda Teal professionally and Mrs. Cody when she's at home with me on Campion Lane, officially had almost nothing to do with the newspaper where she had once been news editor. She still worked for the parent company of the *Observer*, in an office at the newspaper, but under recently changed circumstances.

Lynda had moved up to Grier Ohio NewsGroup, the Buckeye State outpost of the far-flung Grier Media Corp., a few years back to a newly-created post as news coach to both the newspapers and the TV stations. She was also a wiz at digital tie-ins. But in a troubled landscape for news organizations, Grier had done so well that it had attracted the attentions of a corporate raider. Klaus Habsburg-Bonhaus, an Austrian takeover tycoon known as the Tin Man (possibly because he had no heart), had made a hard run at Grier. To fend him off, Grier had split into two companies, Grier Broadcasting Co. and Grier Newspaper Group.

In other words, Grier management had dodged the bullet by shooting the company in the foot instead of waiting for the raider to do it. But I shouldn't complain. Lynda sold some of her Grier stock, on my advice, at a healthy profit while the Tin Man was rattling his tin sword. I had to assure her it wasn't insider trading because I had no special knowledge. I just read *The Wall Street Journal.*

In today's media environment, editors have almost disappeared, so Lynda was lucky to still have a job at Grier Newspaper Group's North Central Division. Working with long-time mentor Megan Whitlock, another survivor, she was negotiating media partnerships with broadcasting companies. Both TV4 and Channel 11 in Cincinnati were in her sights, although she preferred the latter. More recently she'd come up with the idea of a podcast.

"An Ohio newspaper, which shall remain nameless because Grier doesn't own it, got 430,000 downloads on Soundcloud in less than a month with a podcast about an obscure unsolved murder," Lynda had enthused to me in explaining her brainstorm in that direction. "It was number three on iTunes' list of top podcasts nationally. Think of what we could do with one of Mac's high-profile cases!"

Although Lynda had no experience in audio, she planned to do the connecting narration herself. No doubt her husky voice would contribute to the podcast's success. I'd listen for that alone! Megan and Megan's bosses had bought the concept. Now Lynda's biggest problem was picking which McCabe murder victim to build the inaugural episode around—the movie actor, the international con-artist, the mystery writer, the book store owner, or one of the others. She still hadn't decided.

And it wouldn't be long before she would be going on maternity leave with the twins, who were due to join their big sister Donata (age sixteen months) in September. The podcast project would be her swan song for a while, or maybe even her last hurrah. The jury was still out on whether she would go back to the daily paycheck post-partum or concentrate on *Bluegrass*, her family novel-in-progress about bourbon barons and horse breeders in Kentucky. She had time to make up her mind.

The decision from the Historic Conservation Board came down on Monday, May 15, the day after that Mother's Day cooking disaster (mine) that I would rather forget about. The board denied the requested certificate, thereby saying no to the Bijou demolition. Their rationale cited in part the availability of state tax credits for historic properties that could help make a rebirth of the theater possible.

The post-disaster smell had not quite dissipated at Chez Cody by dinner time, so we decided to have a celebratory meal with Mac and Kate at The Speakeasy gastropub—hold the alcohol for Lynda and bring me a Caffeine-Free Diet Coke. We were just about to order a low-calorie dessert when Lynda got a text.

"Did any of you ever hear of a Manny Templeton?" she asked, looking up from the screen.

"The name is unfamiliar to me," Mac rumbled. Kate and I echoed the negative.

"Johanna tells me she's got a hot story running tomorrow," Lynda explained. "This Templeton guy tipped her that City Council members supporting Davenport have been violating Ohio's open meetings law by discussing the Bijou and other stuff via text. And she nailed it."

Lynda spoke with obvious pride in her protégé. Tall Rawls had lived up to Lynda's journalistic motto: "If you don't want it printed, don't do it."

"But the Bijou debate is over now," Kate said.

"Far from it, my dear," her husband informed her. "Not only can the Zoning Board of Appeals overrule the Historic Conservation Board, so can City Council. This exposé of City Hall shenanigans could be significant as the drama continues to play out."

Chapter Six
No Sunshine

Mac and I were still chewing over this the next day in his office when Saylor-Mackie stopped by to make sure he wasn't enjoying a cigar. Shortly after becoming executive vice president and provost, she had made it clear that the campus-wide prohibition on smoking applied to her old friend Sebastian McCabe as well as to lesser mortals. And she made it sick, unlike Ralph's fruitless attempts in the same direction. Have I mentioned that I love that woman?

"Did you see the story in the *Observer* about some City Council members violating the state sunshine law?" I asked her.

She winced. "Gulliver called my attention to it over bacon and eggs this morning. He was quite gleeful about it."

Johanna Rawls had verified her tip from the interested citizen by filing a request to see Erin City Council members' texts under Ohio statue §149.43, familiarly known to journalists as the Open Records Law. Some City Hall functionary had responded with unaccustomed alacrity, coughing up the material in hours instead of days or even weeks. The texts thus uncovered showed Bruce Gordon and four other Council members agreeing that the Bijou should bite the dust and the riverfront bike trail should get extended, as per Hunter Davenport's vision. "We have the votes!" Gordy had crowed.

Johanna's story quoted from the Ohio Supreme Court's website summary of the relevant Buckeye State law, to wit: "A private, prearranged discussion of public business by a majority of a public body's members either face-to-face or by other means such as telephone, e-mail, text or tweet violates the Ohio Open Meetings Act."

I'm not too good on numbers without dollar signs, but even I knew that five Council members out of eight made for a majority.

"I am sure that such a thing would never have happened under your wise mayoral administration," Mac said to Saylor-Mackie. If there was an element of unaccustomed sarcasm in the comment, chalk it up to the Provost's tobacco taboo. Sebastian McCabe was forced to occupy his hands by manipulating a deck of cards instead of smoking a cigar. He made the ace of hearts come up again and again after each reshuffling.

"And why were they being so secretive anyway?" I added. "That brawl over the St. Patrick's Day parade last year took place during Council's regular meeting in front of half the town."

The Provost disabused me of my naivety. "The difference, Jeff, is that any action Council takes on the Bijou building will have significant real-world consequences, unlike the meaningless resolution about the parade. Plus, Davenport's project will be a campaign issue in November, no matter which way it goes in the end."

"Our friend Johanna is to be saluted for recognizing the value of the information she received and pursuing the story," Mac said.

Her front-page story had quoted Manny Templeton throughout. That was no surprise; Tall Rawls wouldn't have bandied about his name, even to Lynda, if he'd been a secret source. The article also included weasel-worded comments from three of the five miscreants on Council, semi-apologizing and promising more transparency in the future. Bruce Gordon and ally Cooper Ralston, however, were nowhere to be found. Reverend Sutterlee, speaking from the other side of the fence, expressed shock that Council members had gone behind his back. Non-incumbent candidates for Council quickly agreed with him, as quoted by Johanna.

I asked Saylor-Mackie whether she bought into Johanna's portrait of Templeton in the story as a civic-minded citizen.

"Take that with a very large grain of salt," she advised. "Most likely he has an angle of some kind. I've known more than one or two self-described 'activists' in my time. It's amazing how often the good of the community happens to coincide with their own self-interest or hobby horse. But maybe I'm just too cynical."

I doubt it.

"I'm not surprised that Bruce is in the thick of this. He was a thorn in my side the whole seven years I was mayor, and he's more devious than you might think from his in-your-face persona. Now he's made this big flip-flop on the Bijou issue, so something's going on there with him."

"A politician who changes his stance is principled and courageous only to those who agree with the change," Mac pontificated. "No doubt that is why I view Bruce Gordon as a perfidious, dishonorable scoundrel for recanting his opposition to Mr. Davenport's ambitions."

"Follow the money," I said unoriginally. "I wouldn't be surprised if Ben Silverstein is doing just that—working on a story about contributors to Gordy's mayoral campaign. In fact, I'd bet on it." *And I only bet after the race is over.* "You know he'll be looking for the initials 'Hunter Davenport' all over the campaign finance report." As news editor of the *Observer & News-Ledger*, a small-town paper, Bernard J. Silverstein (his formal byline) continued to cover local government and even still dabbled in crime news when he could find an excuse.

Saylor-Mackie nodded. "And I'm sure that's just what he'll find. Davenport would regard that money as a business investment. In the short term, Bruce could be a key vote on Council if the Bijou business winds up in their collective lap—which might happen no matter how the Zoning Board of Appeals rules. And in the long-term, Bruce is the most likely of the three mayoral candidates to see development issues Davenport's way."

"The plot machinations of grand opera seem positively guileless by comparison!" Mac said.

That line seemed particularly apt to me later in the week, Thursday, when we attended the premiere of the Erin Opera Company's *Claudette* at the Lyceum. That was the day the Zoning Board of Appeals decreed that the Historic Conservation Board's decision against issuing a certificate of appropriateness for demolition was "not backed by a preponderance of the evidence" and that Davenport Development Co. would suffer severe economic damage if the demolition were not approved. The Board of Appeals also challenged the Conservation Board's argument that historic tax credits would be available to restore the Bijou.

The plan to level the old theater was back on.

Chapter Seven
People Show

With defeat thus snatched from the jaws of victory, I knew Mac would not be in the best of moods when we set out for our night at the opera.

Lynda wasn't exactly chipper, either.

"I wish I could fit into that little black dress you bought me last year," she complained as we dressed to go out. "It would be perfect for the opera." She patted her double baby bump, which had significantly altered her womanly shape. Her admirable curves had been thrown a curve, much more so than in her first pregnancy.

"But you look gorgeous." I meant it. Lynda's oval face with the cutely crooked nose looked radiant, somewhat enhanced by her pout. She wore a Cherokee red maternity dress, matching the color of her nails, lips, and high heels. A diaphanous gold scarf would keep the chill off her bare shoulders if it got cool later. Her honey-blond hair was pinned up in a chic chignon. The intoxicating smell of her perfume, Cleopatra VII, wafted my way and drew me closer.

"I look like your Beetle, except that I'm not green," she complained just as I was about to whisper sweet nothings in her ear.

"Hey, I love that old car."

Apparently, that was the wrong thing to say to a woman carrying twins, judging by the murderous look she gave me. I attempted to make up for the gaffe with non-verbal reassurances of my affection—canoodling, Mac calls it. I guess you could say I was making wanted advances, judging by her response. Consequently, we were a little late meeting Mac and Kate at their house on Half Moon Street. The oldest McCabe child, Rebecca, had volunteered to play with Donata for the evening.

Lynda loves opera like I love my VW – and her. "It has everything but moderation," she'd once instructed me. "There's singing, music, grand costumes, elaborate staging, and drama—or, rather, melodrama. Soap operas really are just like operas, except that they go on for years and don't have music. Operas are always about love and lust. And from what I've seen, so are opera singers." She said the last in a disdainful tone, perhaps thinking of her mother's well-documented appetites along those lines.

On another occasion, Lynda offered the opinion that Jordan Webster should have mounted a production of Verdi's *Falstaff*, with Mac in the title role. "It would be great typecasting." That sally had elicited a completely unironic response from my rotund brother-in-law that his singing wasn't up to the role.

Webster had opted instead to look for a new work. Rebecca's younger sister, almost-sixteen Amanda, had submitted *Starship Mayflower*. ("It's a space opera, Uncle Jeff.") Disappointed that it wasn't chosen for production, she nevertheless joined us to see *Claudette*.

The five of us piled into Mac's criminally huge, fire-engine red 1959 Chevy. Looking at the tail fins on that vehicle still makes me hear the music from *Jaws* in my head, even though he's been driving it for more than a decade.

As Mac turned the car keys over to a parking lot attendant, with whom we would get more acquainted later, I saw a lone figure carrying a picket sign in front of the Lyceum.

"I wonder what that's all about," Lynda said, pulling out her phone to take a picture in case an *Observer* reporter had arrived too late to see it.

The picketer, to my distinct lack of surprise, was Trotskyite mayoral candidate Lani Alvarez. She must buy those signs by the dozen. The hand-lettered message on this one, scrawled with an appropriately red felt marker, said, **"DOWN WITH CULTURAL APPROPRIATION."**

"We missed you at the hearing on the Bijou demolition," I told Alvarez as we came abreast of her.

"That's a bourgeois issue," she sneered. "I'm here to protest an opera about the Cajun people written by a non-Cajun author and starring non-Cajun actors."

Alvarez had straightened her curly black hair and dyed it yellow since the last time I'd seen her, which seemed like cultural appropriation to me. But I keep my job in part by keeping my mouth shut at certain times, and this was one of the times. One of the provisos of the St. Benignus University settlement with Alvarez was the standard stipulation that she would say nothing negative about the university going forward and vice versa.

"Nice tie, Cody," she added.

My Frank Lloyd Wright neckwear matched the color of Lynda's dress, etc., and was set off by a classic blue blazer (gold buttons) over gray trousers. If that doesn't sound dressy enough for the opera, you haven't been to one lately. Dress codes are so twentieth century! Kate had donned a very nice black and silver dress, and Mac clothed his Falstaffian girth in a light gray pinstripe suit and a plaid bow tie, but the lobby of the Lyceum that night was filled with folks in all manner of wardrobe. I spotted capris, stiletto heels, tattoos, orange hair, extreme cleavage, fedoras, mini-dresses, sandals, tuxedos, and polo shirts. Whether in Erin or in Cincinnati or in Rome, studying the audience at an opera is an unequaled people show.

Bruce Gordon, for example, sported bright yellow suspenders I hadn't seen before. Mac sauntered over to him, with me in tow.

"Well, Mr. Gordon, I am pleased to see there is one theater in Erin that you continue to support," he said.

"One is plenty," Gordy snapped back.

"Your perfidy continues to astound me."

"My what?"

Google it, Gordy.

"And perhaps even worse, you prevaricated at the Conservation Board when you said you were coerced into signing that advertisement in the *Observer*. Your mendacity is exceeded only by your gall. If you had a conscience, it would be bothering you."

Bruce Gordon looked at the drink in his hand, then at Mac, then at the small crowd of faces looking his way. Apparently deciding there were more votes in *not* watering Mac's bearded face with his whiskey neat, he stalked off without another word.

"Wrong time, wrong place," I muttered to Mac. "Behave yourself and don't do that again."

My brother-in-law had the grace to look chastened, a rarity. I turned my attention elsewhere.

The proud composer and librettist Luther Kressel was surrounded by well-wishers, including Fr. Pirelli, Fr. Juan Diego Ortega of Campus Ministries, and my old boss, Ralph Pendergast. The *Observer*'s Henry Knox Wilcox, like Amanda apparently bearing no grudge that his own opera submission had lost out to Luther's, was among those gathered around.

Never completely off the clock, I pulled out my smartphone and tweeted: *Big night for SBU professor @LutherKressel! Opening of his exciting new opera, "Claudette."*

The audience mingling in the spacious lobby, where a variety of drinks were being sold, chatted about the weather, opera, the latest turn in the Bijou saga, Erin Eagles baseball, and city politics. Everywhere I looked I saw familiar faces. Serena Mason chatted with Amy Quong, Erin's most charming banker, and with Popcorn. My assistant's main (and only) squeeze, Police Chief Oscar Hummel, was conspicuous by his absence not just from the trio but from the whole event. I suspected that he was home watching TV. Johanna (I was the only one who called her "Tall") Rawls held hands with her much shorter boyfriend, a five-foot-six dental hygienist named Seth Miller. Her aqua dress, nicely setting off her straight blond hair and blue eyes, was also short.

"That's Manny Templeton, the guy who blew the whistle on City Council," Johanna whispered to Lynda, pointing with her plastic cup at a young man who appeared to be under thirty and trying in vain to grow a mustache. With fair hair that badly needed cutting and combing, he looked like he'd just rolled out of bed and needed caffeine. I later realized that he always looked like that. The young woman with whom he was talking, by contrast, carried herself like someone about to go into a boardroom—dark blue skirt, white blouse, chin-length brunette hair.

"So how did Templeton know about the shenanigans at City Hall?" Kate asked.

Good question, given that he looked like he'd have trouble finding the bathroom in that august building.

"I couldn't say," Tall Rawls replied.

"Confidentiality," I said wisely.

"It would be if I knew," the journalist said, "but I don't know. Templeton refused to tell me where he got the info. But it doesn't matter because I confirmed it by getting ahold of those texts. You would think that politicians would know better than to put that kind of stuff in writing, especially on city-issued smart phones."

"It does beggar belief," Mac agreed. "And one remains curious as to Mr. Templeton's source of intelligence about the goings-on at City Hall. He is a hitherto unknown actor in the Bijou drama."

That "one" would be Sebastian McCabe. For myself, I was much more interested in the arrival at that

moment of Nadine Lattimore, God's gift to Channel 11—
and to Erin, for that matter. Everything I'd heard about her
was positive, and she certainly didn't throw off any vibes to
the contrary as she smiled and chatted with a gaggle of
admirers. Either the friendliness was real, or she should
have won an Emmy for acting instead of for newscasting.

This was the first time I'd run into her in person.
Those *Live@11 on TV11* billboards of her and her attractive
co-anchor plastered all over the Channel 11 viewing area
didn't do justice to her classically beautiful face and smooth
skin. Even close-up she didn't look her age, which had to be
pushing forty—just slightly younger than me. The twenty
years or so since she'd been Miss Ohio wore lightly upon
her. She was dressed in a stylish cocktail dress of some soft
gray material, backless with a neckline that was intriguingly
low but not plunging.

Lynda tugged on my arm. "Put your tongue back in
your mouth, darling."

"I only have eyes for you, my dear."

"I'm over here."

My hard-driving wife quickly reminded me about
her attempts to land either Channel 11 or TV4, Cincinnati's
two top-rated stations, into a partnership deal with the Grier
Newspaper Group, North Central Division. "Ms. Lattimore
and I could wind up on the same team."

Play ball!

But I didn't hold the thought. The warning lights
flickered, and Lynda and I, along with the rest of the crowd,
made our way to our seats without me getting any closer to
Erin's homegrown anchorwoman.

On the way into the performance hall we were
handed copies of the program, which Kate had designed.
Dramatically illustrated with color images of Mardi Gras
masks and the Erin Opera Company logo, the cover boldly
proclaimed the Davenport Development Co. as season
sponsor. Was there no way I could get away from

Davenport? But, on the other hand, where was he? I hadn't seen him in the lobby clinging to his beauteous wife.

The stage of the Lyceum, originally designed for Odd Fellows ceremonies, didn't come with an orchestra pit. Instead, as we mounted to our elevated seats, we saw and heard a dozen or so musicians tuning up their flutes, clarinets, timpani, violins, violas, and whatnot on the floor in front of the raised stage. Their conductor—one Stanislaw Kroskof, according to the highly informative program—was an elderly gent, tall but stooped, with white hair all over the place like Albert Einstein. He wore tails.

When the curtain went up, I was impressed at how my big sister and her cohorts had nicely captured the feel of New Orleans with a set design featuring Spanish moss. But I knew that the big splash would come with the costumes at the Mardi Gras ball later in the first act and again at the end of the second. Then all the singers and the extras, known as "supernumeraries," would be wearing dramatic masks created by Kate.

In the opening scenes, however, I spotted a host of friends among the supernumeraries—from the assistant police chief, L. Jack Gibbons, to my favorite nun, Lynda's diminutive gal pal Sister Mary Margaret Malone (AKA Sister Polly, but I usually call her Triple M). SBU's own Kendric Armstrong had a prominent non-speaking role as one of the chief villain's murderous minions. He didn't have to do a thing with his gray pony tail to look the part.

Because Erin was an operatic backwater, most of the singers were young. I noticed in the program that many had studied with Jordan Webster at the University of Wisconsin-Madison School of Music. According to Kate, Webster had sung chorus in several states before spotting Erin as an opera opportunity. Before his arrival in town, Erinites with a taste for something in the musical line more classical than *Annie Get Your Gun* had to drive at least forty-five minutes on a low-traffic day to get it.

Even though the opera was in English, I had trouble following the words. But the synopsis in the program helped me follow the action:

New Orleans, 1850s

Monique LaFarge is a young woman, 17 years old, of a good family. Her parents want her to marry Jean-Christophe de Lubac, scion of another prominent Cajun dynasty. But she is in love with the pirate Pierre Remaux. She has agreed to meet him at a Mardi Gras ball and steal away with him.

Her maid, Marie, overhears the plot and betrays Monique's plans to de Lubac. Desiring both Monique and her family connections, de Lubac is outraged at the idea of being supplanted by a pirate. He sends four ruffians to dispatch his rival. While Remaux heroically battles the killers, de Lubac appears at the ball dressed as Satan in a costume and mask stolen from the pirate. Monique falls for the deception and runs away with him, believing him to be her lover. A seriously wounded Remaux arrives at the ball to find her gone. Assuming she has flown willingly into the arms of another, he sings a sad aria about his love's betrayal and then dies of his wounds.

De Lubac makes love to Monique while still wearing the mask of the devil, then reveals his true identity and tells her that her pirate is dead. In a stirring aria venting her anger, she cries that she is leaving New Orleans, never to return, but vows that de Lubac—who is Satan indeed—will pay for his unspeakable crime.

And that was just the first act! The title character didn't appear until the second.

By the time the curtain went down on Act One, Lynda was in serious need of a dry handkerchief. I provided it, not having used my own. Call me heartless. But I did enjoy it.

Lynda loved it, and so did Amanda McCabe, who mused that perhaps space pirates would add some panache to her *Starship Mayflower*. I could almost see her start the re-write in her head.

At the intermission, during which I was pleased to see Caffeine-Free Diet Coke on offer, I noticed Serena Mason engaged in what might politely be called dialogue with Nadine Lattimore. Their body language said they weren't on the same wavelength.

"I bet Serena's sharing her thoughts about Davenport's Bijou project," I told Mac. "How would you like to be a fly on that wall?"

He ignored the rhetorical question. "Mr. Davenport himself is nowhere to be seen. I find his absence rather surprising in as much as he is the presenting sponsor."

"I had the same thought."

"Maybe he's going to attend a later performance," Lynda said.

"And not the world premiere of a new opera made possible by his generous sponsorship?"

"Maybe he's trying to avoid any possible public confrontations with our Save-the-Bijou supporters," Kate suggested.

"Well, that would make sense," Mac said. "Yes, that must be it."

But it wasn't.

The next morning, we learned that Nadine Lattimore had reported returning home from the opera to find Hunter Davenport dead from multiple stab wounds.

Chapter Eight
Appointment with Murder

"You missed a great opera," I assured our old friend Oscar Hummel as Mac and I took over two of the guest chairs in the Chief's office.

"So did Davenport," he quipped.

Oscar vaped on an e-cigarette as he poured Mac a cup of high-test coffee from a Keurig machine. He stocked a box of decaf cappuccino cartridges just for me.

With the paunch of an aging prizefighter and a balding noggin hidden beneath an Erin Eagles baseball cap, Oscar is no Tom Selleck. But to the irreplaceable Popcorn—a widowed grandmother who is, like him, over fifty and overweight—he's a knight in shining armor.

"It's your kind of case, Mac," he said, "what with the high-profile victim. The coroner was so happy at the change of pace from overdose deaths that she moved this one to the top of the stack." Fentanyl-laced heroin has had the Grim Reaper working overtime throughout Ohio for years now. In 2016, our state had the dubious distinction of lagging only West Virginia in drug overdose deaths. And Sussex County didn't get a free pass for being small and partly rural. In fact, rural areas have been hard hit by the opioid crisis. The southern Ohio town of Portsmouth, not so far away from Erin and smaller in size, has been dubbed "the pill mill of America."

"Details, please," Mac said, looking in desperate need of a cigar.

Ben Silverstein's story in the *Erin Observer & News-Ledger* had been short on the fine points because word of the murder came too late to get much into the print edition. Ben's 12-inch story across the top of page one did report Davenport's last tweet, "*Excited by Zoning Board approval! The Bijou Hotel will be fantastic!*" (The media used to preserve people's last words, like Sir Arthur Conan Doyle telling his wife, "You are wonderful," or Frank Sinatra saying, "I'm losing it." Now they report final tweets. Elizabeth Taylor's was about Kim Kardashian.)

The rest of the front page of the paper had been given over largely to opera coverage, which should have pleased Kate and her friend Jordan Webster. A photo of a man identified as Webster wearing the top hat and skull face of a voodoo spirit during the second-act Mardi Gras scene dominated the page, along with a story and "See review, page 6A." The photo of Lani Alvarez holding her picket sign was smaller, but the cutline below spelled her name right and mentioned that she was running for mayor. Henry Knox Wilcox's review lauded the singing but slammed the opera, which I thought was a conflict of interests given that his own effort at a latter-day *Carmen* had been rejected for performance. I made a mental note to tell Lynda so.

She had an important meeting at her office this morning, but I'd promised to keep her posted on what we found out about Davenport's demise from Oscar. "If this isn't cut and dried, a drug-fueled robbery or something like that, it could be the subject of my podcast!" she had enthused.

The *Online Observer* had a little more about the murder than the print, but Mac would want to get it all from Oscar.

"You know that Davenport was stabbed," the Chief said once all our coffee mugs were filled. (Mac's proclaimed **I SEE NO REASON TO ACT MY AGE**.) "I gave that to Silverstein last night. But I didn't tell him how many times. For your information only, the victim was speared twelve times with an approximately eight-inch blade. The killer wasn't kind enough to leave the weapon behind."

"Twelve times!" I exclaimed "Talk about overkill!"

"That's actually not as over-the-top as you might think. Google 'multiple stab wounds' and you'll see what I mean."

"Still, it is safe to say that the killer was not leaving his victim's fate to chance," Mac said, "and that personal animus may have been a factor."

"I thought you wanted facts, not assumptions."

"My apologies, Oscar. Please proceed."

"Right. Davenport told his wife, the Channel Eleven anchorwoman Nadine Lattimore, that he had an appointment with a man named Pinkerton at nine-thirty. Or so she reported. Davenport didn't give the man's first name, but he did use a male pronoun, she said. Ms. Lattimore went to that opera. You guys probably saw her there." That was an assumption, but we acknowledged the correctness of it with nods. "She says she found her husband's body when she got home."

"Surely nine-thirty on a Thursday evening is an odd time for an appointment," Mac said.

"Yeah. That's one of the things I want to ask Ms. Lattimore about. We didn't get into that in the first interview."

"Too bad you don't have this Pinkerton guy on surveillance video," I said.

"We do."

"You do!"

"Yeah. The Davenports have quite a security system. But you can't tell anything useful from the video. You wouldn't even know it's a man if you didn't know it was a man." *I think I followed that.* "The subject is slender, or at least not heavy, wearing a cap over long hair that could be a wig, dark glasses, a full beard. He never shows his full face to the camera, like maybe he knew it was there. The time stamp on the video confirms that he rang the doorbell at a couple of minutes shy of nine-thirty."

"That name Pinkerton could be a phony, taken from the name of the famous detective agency," I posited.

"That's a good bet, since there's nobody of that last name residing in Sussex County that we can find."

Mac looked thoughtful, which is the only way he knows how to look. "The name resonates with me as well, albeit in some other context which eludes me."

That context played tag with Mac's mind over the following week, but at that moment all three of us were distracted by the hesitant entrance of Nadine Lattimore.

She wasn't wearing widow's weeds, but she didn't have to. The rings under her green eyes told the tale. Her chestnut hair, while not exactly run riot, hadn't seen much attention that morning. She looked her age, and then some.

"You asked me to come see you, Chief," she said. Her familiar voice sounded dispirited, but not as if she were making a point of it.

Oscar sat up straighter and, in a gentlemanly gesture, doffed his Erin Eagles baseball cap. "Yes, of course. Thanks for coming in, Ms. Lattimore. I know this is a tough time for you. Please have a seat." There was one left.

"How many murders have I covered in my TV news career?" she said as she sat. "But I could never have imagined . . ."

She paused, taking in the audience. Oscar, who is no Sherlock Holmes but also not oblivious to body language, picked up her surprise that Mac and I hadn't made a gracious exit.

"This is Professor Sebastian McCabe and Thomas Jefferson Cody, both of St. Benignus University," he said, impressing me by hauling out my full moniker. "I hope you don't mind if they stay. We're a small department and they've sometimes been of help to me on especially tough cases."

"How could I forget?" the widow said with a touch of humor and a sly look at Mac. "Professor McCabe once unmasked a murderer live on a rival station. That depressed my ratings for a month. He was also more recently a major stumbling block to my husband's first major development project with his Save-the-Bijou campaign."

"No building, however treasured, is a fraction as important as a human life," Mac said, tritely but sincerely. "You have my heartfelt condolences on the death of your husband."

"Thank you."

I chimed in with my own expression of sympathy, trying to avoid sounding like I was on autopilot. That's not easy. What can you say that's original at a time like that?

"Coffee?" Oscar asked.

"Yes, please. Black."

"Pick your poison." Oscar pointed to a tray full of cartridges in assorted flavors and brand names. Within a minute or so his guest was sipping on a cup of Cavendish's Dark Roast, her shapely legs crossed.

Then the Chief got down to business. "You were at the opera at the Lyceum last night during the time of your husband's death, right?"

"That depends on when he died. I didn't stay for the whole opera."

"You didn't?" Oscar braced himself with a sip of java from his Cincinnati Reds mug.

"No. I co-anchor both the five o'clock and the eleven o'clock newscasts, and the eleven o'clock report with Germaine Davis is the ratings leader. We're the only two female co-anchors in the state. But it was so exciting to premiere a new opera right here in Erin that I wanted to be present on the opening night. *Claudette* started at eight. I arrived in time to mingle a bit in the lobby before the curtain went up, but I left after the first act to go to work. I'd planned to see the second act on Sunday afternoon. I guess I still will."

Mac raised an eyebrow. The widow didn't have much of an alibi, given that stabbing a guy to death wasn't a time-intensive activity. She could have been the visitor in disguise. Intermission was about 9:15, which would have given her plenty time to get to their home in the country by 9:30ish. Then she could have floored it afterwards to get to Cincinnati, where her exact arrival time at Channel 11 likely wouldn't have been noted anyway. If Mac wasn't thinking all of those things, he should turn in his junior detective badge.

"We don't have an official time of death yet from the coroner," Oscar said, "and when we do, it will be within a range of a few hours. But as a working theory, it seems reasonable that it happened between the time this Pinkerton person entered your home at nine-twenty-eight and when he left seven minutes later."

"Then I would have been on my way to the studio while Hunter was being . . ." She stopped, swallowed, then downed some coffee, holding the mug in a death grip.

"I was rather surprised at your husband's absence from your side at the opera," Mac observed. "As you said, it was a world premiere and he—or, rather, his development business—was the presenting sponsor not only for *Claudette* but for the opera company's entire season."

She allowed herself a Mona Lisa smile. "Hunter didn't really like opera, Professor."

"Oh? Then why sponsor it?"

"I talked him into it. I love opera. Singing an aria from *Aida* was my talent when I competed in the Miss America pageant, though I didn't have the chops to make it as a singer. I was very excited when Jordan launched the Erin Opera Company last year. I convinced Hunter that it would be good business in a town like Erin for him to put his company's name on it as the presenting sponsor this season. That's why he did it. So it was no great sacrifice for him to stay home for this meeting, even on opening night."

"Why was the meeting so late in the evening?" Oscar asked.

Nadine Lattimore shook her head. "I have no idea. I can only assume it was at the request of the visitor. Hunter was in his office at home that afternoon, so presumably he could have met with this person then."

"You told me last night that your husband said he was meeting somebody named Pinkerton, no first name supplied. We have video of somebody, presumably the Pinkerton guy, ringing the doorbell and entering your home. We're going to talk to the neighbors and use social media to try to get a line on him. You said you got the impression from the way your husband talked that this wasn't somebody he'd done business with before. Did he say anything else about Pinkerton?"

"He did tell me one thing." She paused, glanced at Mac, and then came out with it: "He said this man he was meeting had something to tell him—some 'dirt,' as he put it—about Sebastian McCabe."

Chapter Nine
Too Many Suspects

"There are no secrets to be shared about me, I assure you!" Mac protested. "My life is an open book."

Many books, in fact. I wrote them.

Was that a smirk I detected on Oscar's face before he covered it with a sip of coffee?

"Well," the Chief said after the caffeine refuel, "that's certainly interesting. And I presume Mr. Davenport was the sort of guy who would want to get the dirt on an opponent?"

Nadine Lattimore sighed. "My husband grew up poorer than I did, although my family wasn't especially well off. He fought for everything he ever had. I loved him very much, but I have to say that he didn't always play nice. Hunter would be the first to admit that. In his defense, though, he told me that in taking that meeting he just wanted to find out what this Pinkerton's game was. That is the one other thing he said about the meeting. I forgot to mention that."

Mac maintained radio silence, maybe because this was supposed to be Oscar's show. But that wouldn't shut him up for long.

"Let's think this through," Oscar said. "Whoever made that appointment with your husband—presumably the person on the surveillance video—either really had something to tell him about Mac here or he was setting your husband up. Either is theoretically possible. But given the way it turned out, I pick door number two."

"Bravo, Oscar!" Mac enthused. "Your logic is most admirable."

"And that would mean we're dealing with cold-blooded, premeditated murder by somebody who had a reason to kill Hunter Davenport," the Chief continued. "Who do you think would fit that description, Ms. Lattimore?" Mac would have said, "*Cui bono?*" But the question was the same in any language.

The widow turned to my brother-in-law. "No offense, Professor McCabe, but I have to say that you would certainly have a reason."

To my credit, I didn't laugh. But I wanted to. For starters, Oscar had called the figure on the surveillance video "not heavy." That's hardly a description of Sebastian McCabe—au contraire, as he himself might put it.

Mac hiked a quizzical eyebrow. "How so, Ms. Lattimore?"

"To be clear, I'm not accusing you of anything, Professor; I'm just answering the question. With Hunter's death, your cause—which seems very important to you—has won. The Bijou will not be torn down, despite the approval of the Zoning Board. I disagreed with Hunter about that project. Even more importantly, I have no wish to be in the destruction and construction business. I'm going to wind down Davenport Development as soon as I can. I don't know what's going to happen to the Bijou building, except that I will sell it to anyone with a viable plan to enhance the community. I'm sure you and its other defenders will find some noble usage for it."

Was "noble usage" a sarcastic put-down? I'm not sure, even though I consider myself an expert at it. In any case, I had a passing thought that this could be very good news for St. Benignus University. The Provost wanted to bring gown into town, and her husband and Kendric

Armstrong thought an off-campus theater would be a dandy way to do it.

"It would be disingenuous, even hypocritical, to pretend that I am not pleased by this news and very grateful to you," Mac said. "I certainly did not expect this turn of events. You have taken a major decision rather quickly."

"There was no decision, really. My path was clear. I don't know the first thing about running that business, and I wouldn't feel comfortable letting someone else run it."

"You're sure you're Mr. Davenport's only heir, then?" Oscar asked.

This wasn't as silly a question as you might think. In 2013, a woman in Cleveland hired her daughter's boyfriend to kill her husband of four months for his life insurance, not realizing that the husband's ex-wife was still the beneficiary. Major fail!

"I'm sure," the widow replied without hesitation. "Our marriage wasn't a business arrangement, so we didn't have a prenuptial agreement or anything like that, but we did make our wills together. When Hunter and I married fourteen years ago, he was a widower with two children. His son, Barry, died in Afghanistan. His daughter, Julia, is a nun at a cloistered Benedictine abbey in Connecticut. Hunter visited her every Easter and Christmas. At her request, he gave the abbey a donation of several million dollars two years ago in lieu of a bequest in his will. The abbey needed the money sooner rather than later."

From the look on their faces, Mac and Oscar appeared to share my opinion that a cloistered nun did not make a good murder suspect. Nadine Lattimore, on the other hand, fit the role like a hand in a glove (and I don't mean O.J. Simpson's). She could even have been the person on the surveillance video. Wouldn't she know something about makeup and costumes from her work in television? And who would know better than the woman of the house that the camera was there to record her performance? I filed that away under, "To Be Considered Later."

"Back to my question," Oscar said. "Who else might be happy to see your husband dead?"

The former beauty queen ran a hand through her disheveled hair. Her roots were the same natural-looking shade of chestnut as the rest of her hair, which I found notable in a woman who would never see forty again. Her husband's mane I had been less sure about.

"May I have another cup of coffee?"

"Sure thing"

I tried to figure out whether she was stalling for time, sleep-deprived, or just needed the stimulation of more caffeine to help her work on the question, but I never decided. Oscar Kuerigged her up a cup of java and she drank it greedily.

"There's Manny Templeton," she continued after coming up for air, "the guy who raised hell about Council member meeting illegally by text. That was a good news story, but my journalistic instinct tells me that Templeton is not just a concerned citizen. I think he's a front for somebody."

That makes it unanimous.

"For whom, for example?" Mac asked.

"You don't know?" Skepticism was writ large on her lovely face.

"I have no idea, Ms. Lattimore. I keenly wish that I did."

"As soon as I saw the story in the *Observer*, I assumed it was part of a strategy to save the theater."

"It could be," I conceded, "but we had nothing to do with it."

Nadine—it was hard not to think of her that way after all the time she'd spent in my home via TV—nodded slowly. "Okay, then, I'll take your word for that."

"Any other ideas?" Oscar pressed her.

"Wade Pennington, the candy man whose store is next to the Bijou, was furious that the city might take his property by eminent domain for Hunter's project. But I can't believe he'd turn to violence. I remember buying candy from him when I was a kid. I'm sorry, but I can't really believe that anybody would kill Hunter."

"Somebody did, though," Oscar pointed out. His tone of voice took the sting out of it. "Your husband could be tough in business. You said so yourself. That makes enemies."

"I'm not naïve about that, but who kills somebody over a business dispute?"

The Corleone family comes to mind.

"Speaking of business," Mac said, "what about Mr. Davenport's partner? There are many reasons why a partner might prove inconvenient in the extreme." *Whether a partner in business or in romance*, I added to myself.

She hesitated. "He was the only owner of Davenport Development. I wouldn't even let Hunter put my name on the paperwork because I could see that it might create a conflict of interests for me as a journalist at some point."

But I knew what Mac meant.

"Your husband was also the co-owner of a canoe and bike rental operation on Water Street called Paddles & Wheels," I said. "That wasn't his marquee enterprise, but he talked about it at the Conservation Board hearing. And the *Observer* carried a feature story about it later. The other owner is a woman named Sheila something."

"Sheila Paxton," Mac supplied.

"Why bring her into this?" Nadine set down her empty coffee cup with emphasis. "She's so young."

"Twenty-two," I added helpfully.

"Do you know her?" Oscar asked Nadine. Math may not be the Chief's strong suit, but I'm pretty sure he didn't need a calculator to figure out that twenty-two minus the widow's age was a significant spread. Cops are paid to have dirty minds sometimes.

Nadine nodded. "I know her well enough to like her. One of our reporters put together a package on Paddles & Wheels a year or so ago. She's a bright, vivacious young woman who wanted to be her own boss and saw a way to make it happen. But she was at a point where she needed more capital, so I encouraged Hunter to invest in the company. It was an ideal arrangement for both: The additional funds allowed her to expand the company, but she retained majority ownership. That kept Paddles & Wheels eligible for state and local incentives for female-owned businesses." *Aha! Just as I had told Lynda.* "Sheila was very grateful to my husband, as she expressed to me on a number of occasions."

"And yet," Mac mused, "the situation does seem less than perfect from a young entrepreneur's point of view."

"What do you mean?" Oscar asked.

"Ms. Paxton was no longer in complete control. Even a minority partner has clout." Mac should know. He owns part of Mo's Mysteries & Marvels bookstore. But don't tell anybody. "What happens now to your husband's share of that business, Ms. Lattimore?"

"I guess it's mine, unless there was some other arrangement. I haven't really thought about that. Compared to the scope of what Hunter had planned with the development company, the bike and canoe business wasn't that big a deal."

Mac stood up. "You have been most helpful, Ms. Lattimore. Whatever our problems might be on this case, Oscar, a dearth of suspects will not be one of them—quite the opposite, in fact. We seem to have almost too many."

Chapter Ten
Hard Ball Player

Not sure how to put all of that into my promised text update to Lynda as we left Oscar's office, I settled for: *Visited Oscar, talked to widow. More on tap. Meet me later for lunch?* Within 30 seconds, she was back at me with: *You romantic! Make it Daniel's at noon.*

"What's your takeaway on Nadine Lattimore?" I asked Mac, re-holstering my phone.

"I find her pulchritudinous charms aesthetically pleasing, if somewhat distracting."

Translation: She's hot!

"Tell me something I don't know—like whether you think she used her husband for a pin cushion."

Mac shrugged his well-padded shoulders. "She appeared to be sincere in all of her responses, aggrieved by the loss of her husband, and loath to turn our attention to a young woman she admires."

"Yeah, all of that. I liked her."

"As did I, Jefferson. She is a strong and decisive woman—strong enough not to hide her vulnerability. However, we must remember that her profession, at which is she accomplished, requires a measure of acting."

"That did occur to me."

"Well spotted, then! If there were marital discord, infidelity, that sort of thing between her and her late spouse, we can be confident that Colonel Gibbons will uncover it. Therefore, the possibility need not concern us at this point."

Oscar hadn't directly asked any questions along those lines, perhaps also dazzled by Nadine's pulchritudinous charms. Not that she would likely tell him anyway if one of the Davenports was stepping out. But Lt. Col. L. Jack Gibbons, Oscar's unflappable assistant chief and lead investigator, could be counted on to ferret out any relevant gossip. Middle-aged, average in looks, and medium in size, Gibbons is not a show horse but a work horse. While he handled the necessary routine police work in the case, Mac and I would work our way through Nadine's unlikely (my characterization) suspect list.

We found Wade Pennington behind the old wooden counter at the Sweet Shoppe. Mac ordered a pound each of Chunky candy bars, Reese's Peanut Butter Cups, and Mary Janes. That's his idea of health food.

While Pennington weighed it out, Mac said casually, "I suppose you saw the news that our mutual bête noire is no more."

"I shall shed no crocodile tears for Davenport," the candy man said, his round face indeed tear-free. "The way he did business, I'm surprised somebody didn't do him in a long time ago. The man was a heartless out-of-towner. What did it matter to him that the Penningtons have been selling candy on Front Street for a hundred years? We had a sit-down, just he and I, a few days before the Historic Conservation Board hearing. He had the gall to tell me I could just move the shop. See what I mean about no heart?"

"You sound pretty heartless yourself," I opined. "Speak no ill of the dead and all that."

"I feel sorry for his wife, I guess," Pennington admitted. "She seems nice enough—on TV, anyway. I don't know the lady." He popped a Baby Ruth in his mouth. If he had recently lost weight, as I suspected, he seemed determined to find it again. "And it's not like I prayed for his death before bed-time every night. What would be the point? I'm sure the bastard's dead hand will still continue to wreak havoc as his big project goes ahead without him."

"By no means," Mac assured him jovially.

"Eh? What are you talking about, McCabe?"

"We just spoke with Nadine Lattimore a few moments ago. She told us that she has neither the desire nor the business acumen to pursue the Bijou development. The building is saved and, therefore, so is yours."

Pennington blinked a couple of times as that sank in, then he broke into a smile that made his face look like an emoji. "I never expected that! I guess she really is a nice lady, God bless her."

So, no motive for Pennington if he really didn't know that killing Davenport would also kill the hotel project. Except maybe sheer hatred. But when somebody has been stabbed a dozen times, hatred works.

"Where were you last night?" Mac asked.

"Why do you ask?"

"Call it a habit, if you will." *That and the fact that your slimmed-down body could have been the one on the surveillance video.*

"I will. Everybody in Erin knows that you're a regular Sherlock Holmes." *Please don't encourage him.* "I was at a Knights of Columbus meeting last night from seven-thirty to ten-thirty with about twenty or twenty-five brother knights. I'm a Fourth Degree."

This was Greek to me. Not being a joiner, I don't know much about fraternal organizations, not even religious ones. But clearly Pennington was trying to pull rank with this degree business. I was unimpressed.

"Who else do you think is well rid of Hunter Davenport?" I said.

"Why ask me? What makes you think I know anything?"

"I just thought you might be more aware of Davenport's anti-fan club than the average bear. You must have shared a few grumbles here and there."

"Maybe so, but I wouldn't want to get anybody into trouble."

"Not even a killer?" Mac asked.

A grandmotherly type accompanied by two kids old enough to know that candy is bad for them spared Pennington from having to answer for a few minutes while he rang up their order. Mac and I stood patiently to one side until they cleared out of the store.

"Well, Sheila Paxton comes to mind," Pennington said as the door closed behind them, causing a bell to ring. "I mean, objectively speaking."

"Ah, yes, Mr. Davenport's partner in Paddles & Wheels," Mac said.

"Yeah. Regular customer of mine. She loves candy corn all year round, not just in the fall. I forget how the subject came up—maybe she saw my *Save the Bijou* poster— but she vented to me one day about how pissed she was that Davenport wouldn't let her buy him out. It was kind of a 'Shark Tank' deal, where he invested money with the idea that he would also help to grow the company with his business expertise. But the operation still qualifies for government goodies available only to businesses owned by women. Nobody ever handed my family anything like that, but I don't hold it against Sheila. She didn't write the law. Hey, I'm not going to trash a good customer and a fellow small business owner. In fact, I'm sorry I mentioned her. She wouldn't hurt a fly."

If Hunter Davenport had been a fly, we wouldn't be here.

"Does anyone else occur to you as being less than devastated by Mr. Davenport's demise?" Mac asked.

"You might as well get the sign-in sheet from the Conservation Board meeting and go down the list of names. Most of us were there to oppose Davenport."

"But you yourself didn't expect his death to change anything," I objected. At least, that's how he'd acted.

Pennington nodded. "A fair point, but maybe the killer was just after payback." *That's what I thought about you, Wade.* "I wonder if Dr. Hawthorne was mad about the Bijou deal?"

David Hawthorne, DPM, was the husband of Kate's friend Rosalie Gamble Hawthorne, as in Gamble Bank.

"Why should he be?" Mac asked.

"He used to own the Bijou building. From what I hear, he sold it for a song—and not with the idea that it would be torn down for a big development project. If he'd known what Davenport had in mind for the property, he could have held out for a lot more money."

Chapter Eleven
Motive!

Poor Mac had a meeting of some academic committee while I biked over for lunch with Lynda at Daniel's Apothecary. It was a great-to-be-alive day, warm and sunny and perfect for a ride. Daniel's, the old-fashioned soda shop next to the *Erin Observer & News-Ledger* offices, features 1950s decor and such classic menu items as "The Big Bopper Burger." I walked in and found my lady love already seated, sucking an impossibly thick chocolate milkshake through a straw and reading on her phone.

"What's news?" I asked. I had been blissfully ignorant of national and international chaos all morning.

"I'm reading a review of *Claudette* by Grayson Caldwell."

My face must have been a question mark, which Lynda quickly answered:

"He's a famous opera critic."

"Is there more than one?"

"Absolutely, but he's near the top. I can't even guess why he'd come to Erin, but he did and he wrote about the premiere of Luther's opera for the online version of *New York Review*. Want to hear it?"

"Heavens no! Just give me the bottom line, translated from opera-speak."

"It's devastating. He called the Erin Opera Company 'an ambitious but inadequate farm team.'"

"Wait a minute. He used a hackneyed sports metaphor in an opera review?"

She nodded. "Yeah, insult to injury. He actually liked the libretto and the music, but he raked the singers over the coals."

"That's good. I can put out a tweet and a press release touting the thumbs up for Luther's work. Funny, though, this opera maven's reaction was just the opposite that of our buddy Hank Wilcox." He hates being called Hank. "And that reminds me: Wasn't it a conflict of interests for Wilcox to review *Claudette*, given that his own opera was in competition for production and lost out?"

"Hmmm. I never thought of it that way. I'll take it up with Frank."

Somehow, amid all the changes at the *Observer* over the years, Frank Woodford still hung on as the congenial editor and general manager. Not that he exerted a heavy hand in the newsroom. Most of his work was done on the golf course, as far as I could tell.

Lynda pulled on her milkshake. This is one of her favorite indulgences, along with Manhattans at cocktail hour when not pregnant. Normally she keeps the consumption of both in check to keep her curvaceous figure. With twins in the hopper, that consideration was no longer very relevant. She must have seen me mentally calculating the 1,200 calories circulating through her straw.

"I'm eating for three," she snapped.

"I didn't say a word."

"You thought it. But you can make up for that by telling me that the Davenport murder is going to make a really good podcast."

"I can tell you that, but I don't yet know whether it's true. You be the judge." I filled her in on our morning interviews with Oscar, Nadine Lattimore, and Wade Pennington, saving the anchorwoman for the last.

"Wow, so much good material," my beloved enthused. "And if we could snag an interview or two with

Nadine, a near-miss for Miss America, that would really give the podcast a national reach. International, even!"

"Good luck with that."

"You mean because we're competitors in the news business? Don't forget, Megan and I are still in talks to create a strategic partnership between Grier Newspaper Group and Channel Eleven."

"Fine, but I'm not sure she'll be in the mood to talk, even to her own station. Her husband just got skewered like St. Sebastian, Lyn."

She wrinkled her eyebrows in thought. "I think St. Sebastian was martyred by arrows, not knives. Mac would know for sure."

"Still."

"I didn't intend to try talking to her for the podcast right now anyway, darling. We can do it later, when the subject isn't quite so raw. The podcast series won't even begin until the case is solved. Tell Mac to hurry up with that, by the way." *I'll get right on that, my sweet.*

"But I do need to record some of the material while the murder is still a mystery. Everything will change after Mac figures it out, including people's perceptions of what they thought earlier. So, I've got to get cracking with my recorder. I'll want to talk to you and Mac, of course, and some of the suspects. I don't take the candy man seriously as a candidate for killer, but he'd be a great interview."

Lynda typed a note into her phone as she continued without a pause: "What's next for you and Mac?"

"I'm going to sneak out of the office this afternoon." Mac didn't have to sneak, being a full professor. Fortunately, Popcorn is both willing and able to woman the barricades in my absence. I was in the middle of drafting a speech for Fr. Pirelli, but that could wait. "We're going to talk to Sheila Paxton, Davenport's partner in Paddles & Wheels, and David Hawthorne, who used to own the Bijou building."

"You mean Rosalie Hawthorne's husband, the foot doctor?"

"That's the one."

"I've been thinking about making an appointment with him."

"You could do that. Or you could stop wearing four-inch heels until after the babies are born."

"If I want medical advice . . ."

And so forth.

Lynda did eventually visit Dr. Hawthorne in a professional capacity—his profession, not hers—but that came later. She was tied up on a conference call with her out-of-town boss, Megan Whitlock, when Dr. Hawthorne found a few moments to talk to Mac and me that afternoon before a round of cutting off corns or whatever.

The podiatrist was in his late forties, older than me and about the same age as his wife. I'd heard that he and Rosalie had been high school sweethearts, in fact. He peered at us over a pair of half-moon glasses as we sat across from him in one of the patient rooms.

"You said you wanted to talk to me about the history of the Bijou," he began, although we already knew that. Mac had decided to put a fig leaf over our real reason for talking to a man who was almost certainly an innocent bystander. "Why the interest now? I thought the controversy was a dead issue with the ruling from the Zoning Board of Appeals. Or is City Council going to step in?"

"There is no need for that," Mac confided. "Ms. Lattimore has decided to shelve the plan to demolish the historic edifice now that her husband has passed away." *Speaking of dead issues.* "Therefore, the history of the building becomes newly relevant now that it has a future as well as a past."

Hawthorne smiled. "That's wonderful!"

"Indeed it is. And as an advocate for saving the building, I feel a responsibility to be part of that future." That was even true, as Mac had commented to me on the way to the doc's office.

"You sound pretty happy about the turn of events, considering that you sold Davenport the building at a bargain price, from what we understand," I told Hawthorne. Without intending to, I had become Bad Cop.

He shrugged. "It seemed like a good idea at the time. Actually, my wife is the one who sold the building. It had been in her family a long time. When Rosalie inherited it, I toyed with the idea of restoring the building as a performance theater—for the Erin Opera Company, as a matter of fact. I love opera! I'm seeing *Claudette* on Sunday. But Lafcadio Figg, who revived the Lyceum, convinced me that idea was a non-starter—at least for me. After all, I'm a doctor, not a developer." *Damn it, Jim! I'm a doctor not a . . .* Hawthorne must have grown up on re-runs of the original *Star Trek*. "These days it seems like people are coming out of the woodwork with ideas for the building, but that wasn't the case a year ago when Rosalie sold it."

"So you weren't angry with Davenport for potentially making a fortune off the building your wife sold him?" I pressed.

He looked blank. "What? Are you kidding? Why should I be? It's not like I'm out anything. I couldn't have done what Davenport was planning to do, or what anybody else might do. Hell, he took a white elephant off our hands. How are your feet, by the way? Any problems?"

Sheila Paxton didn't have the figure of a woman with a candy corn jones, which just adds to the mound of evidence that life is unfair. She was slim, athletic, and muscular, with chin-length brunette hair and a friendly manner. All that biking and canoeing apparently had paid off in healthful vitality. Dressed in white shorts and a yellow *Paddles & Wheels* tank top, she barely looked her age of 22.

We caught up with her at the store on Water Street, surrounded by bicycles much newer than the Schwinn that takes me most places I want to go. Rental rates ranged from $6 for one hour to $50 for all day. The canoes were in the water. Lynda, liberated from her conference call, met us there to do her first recording for the podcast.

Lynda asked most of the questions this time, while Mac and I stood around like potted plants. She explained the concept of the true crime podcast, and how she wanted to talk to the young entrepreneur about her business partner's death. Without emphasizing the word, I noticed that she was careful to say *business* partner.

"And mentioning Paddles & Wheels will be good publicity," Lynda said as the clincher to her spiel. "People all over the world could potentially hear it if it goes viral." Not that people all over the world would be renting bikes and canoes in Erin.

"I don't mind talking about it," Ms. Paxton said, "but I'm still a little shook up. You don't expect somebody you know to be murdered. And it must have happened while I was at the opera."

The penny dropped and I remembered seeing her in the lobby of the Lyceum, looking much different in a dark blue skirt and white blouse. "You were talking to Manny Templeton at the opening-night reception," I blurted.

"I was? Who's that?"

"The civic benefactor who's been making a fuss about certain City Council members, Davenport supporters, flouting the sunshine law via text. It was in the *Observer*."

"I don't subscribe." Lynda's lovely oval face contorted into a frown. Ms. Paxton didn't seem to notice. "But I do remember a guy yammering on that night about lack of transparency at City Hall. He looked like he combed his hair with an eggbeater." *Yep, that was Templeton.*

Lynda cranked up her digital recorder and started asking Sheila questions, beginning with her name for the record. Then she moved quickly on:

"How well did you know your late business partner, Hunter Davenport?"

"Not as well as you might think. My father once told me never to go into business with a friend. Mr. Davenport wasn't a friend; he was a customer, to begin with. The store was only a few weeks old when he stopped in one day to rent a bike and saw potential for growth. Within fifteen minutes he was imagining a bicycle trail going all the way to West Virginia and adding canoe rentals. I didn't have the money for expansion at that point, but he had it and he was willing to risk it. We tripled the number of bikes for rent and launched a big ad campaign that caused a significant increase in rentals. That's just the beginning if Mr. Davenport's bike trail plans work out."

This was familiar territory from the *Observer* feature on Sheila Paxton. As a biking enthusiast, I mentally added a lonely checkmark to the deceased's positive column.

"Mr. Davenport's proposal for the Bijou Theatre site made a lot of enemies who saw him as a hard-hearted businessman," Lynda observed. "I gather you saw a softer side of him."

Ms. Paxton shifted uncomfortably. "Well, no. I can't honestly say that I saw any softness there. Maybe his wife did, if anybody. But he was a good businessman and he provided the capital when I needed it. Bankers only give you money when you don't need it."

Mac cleared his throat with a theatrical rumble and slipped Lynda a note.

"Word about town is that you were angry that Mr. Davenport refused to let you buy him out," she read aloud.

"About town? You mean I'm the subject of gossip? Wow! That's kind of cool. Okay, yeah, I was furious for a while. I wanted full control of the business and I thought now that I had a track record Gamble Bank might be willing to lend me the money to buy Mr. Davenport out. But our buy-sell agreement didn't give me the right to do that just because I wanted to. He had to agree to it.

"I was pissed at first when he refused. He said Paddles & Wheels was poised to benefit big time from development along the river and he was in it for the long haul. After I thought about it from his point of view, I could see his point and I started to simmer down. When I looked at it rationally I realized that he took a chance on me when it mattered. I really have nothing to complain about— especially now."

"What do you mean?" Lynda asked.

"Well, now that he's dead, the buy-sell agreement gives me the right to buy his share from Ms. Lattimore. And since Mr. Davenport and I insured each other's lives as part of the partnership deal, I have the money to do that."

Chapter Twelve
Grasping at Straws

"I can't believe she spilled that for the podcast," Lynda said as we hit the sidewalk. "What a motive!"

"And yet," mused Mac as he paused to light a cigar, "her willingness to speak of it so candidly would seem to indicate an unburdened conscience."

"Unless that's just what she wants us to think!"

At that unarguable retort from my energized wife, we parted company. Lynda went to pick up Donata, and I went back to campus with Mac for a quick stop at the office to close out the week. I knew there was no crisis at work because that would have already made its way to my smartphone.

"Hot date this weekend?" I asked Popcorn.

She unconsciously primped her dyed blond hair. "Oscar's taking me to a Reds game in Cincinnati tomorrow night."

"You crazy kids. Don't forget your pepper spray in case he gets too frisky."

She whacked me with a rolled-up copy of *The Spectator*, the SBU student newspaper, on her way out the door.

A Saturday morning in mid-May would usually find Lynda playing softball with Triple M and a group of regular co-conspirators, but she was no longer built for that. So, we started the day with a leisurely perusal of the *Erin Observer & News-Leader* at the breakfast table. There was plenty to peruse.

"Ha!" I shouted with the second section of the paper in one hand and a cup of defanged coffee in the other. "I knew it."

"What's that, darling?" Lynda was helping Donata eat her cereal while also skimming through the other part of the paper. Newspaper-reading moms learn to do that if the prefer the paper version of the paper.

"Da!" our daughter added, extending her little fist toward me and spilling chewed Cheerios out of her mouth. She can say six words, and that is my favorite one. Her hair started out red, like mine, but was now tending toward strawberry blond.

"Ben Silverstein has a story about contributions to Bruce Gordon's campaign for mayor, just as I predicted," I boasted. "Gordy didn't change his position on the Bijou development because he had a sudden enlightenment about the virtues of building a new hotel on Front Street. Campaign cash changed hands."

"You mean from Davenport to Gordon?"

"Of course! That must have been it, though you can't prove anything by the less-than-transparent campaign finance reports filed so far."

I summarized what I'd just been reading:

Bruce Gordon's mayoral campaign had received contributions totaling $49,500 from 45 limited liability companies, familiarly known as LLCs. For a small-town mayoral campaign, that was not chump change. It was also perfectly legal. Although corporations aren't allowed to donate to candidates in Ohio, LLCs are. A limited liability company is a business structure that does what it sounds like—limits the liability of the owner—but isn't a corporation.

The owners of the LLCs donating to the Gordon for Mayor Committee—companies with unrevealing names like Paragon Properties, the View-Halloo Organization, and Acme Enterprises—weren't identified in the campaign finance reports, according to Ben's story. But they all had the same address on Walnut Street, which Ben noted also housed "the small office of the fledgling Davenport Developments." And all the contributions had come after Gordy showed up at the Historic Preservation Board meeting with his impersonation of Judas on May 3.

Appropriately, Ben quoted the feisty florist's mayoral opponents weighing in on the LLC contributions. Reginald "Scrappy" Fortesque III called them "shocking and unconscionable." He himself had reported no campaign contributions, not even a few dollars, according to Ben. For Lani Alvarez the dark money was "typical capitalist election-buying, which will breathe its last gasp in this town with my election." Her own coffers held $4,527 in checks from socialists, Green Party affiliates, and SBU's Kendric Armstrong. That last stung me. Didn't the man realize that his candidate had once sued our mutual employer? Where was the loyalty?

Ben Silverstein's attempts to get Gordy to confirm the identity of the individual behind the multiple LLCs had so far proved fruitless: "Gordon did not respond to phone calls, e-mails, and tweets from the *Observer & News-Ledger*," the veteran journalist reported. Hunter Davenport was, of course, permanently unavailable to respond to questions about Davenport Development's shared address with Gordy's generous donor(s). Maybe that's why the story only rated the second section front, promoted with a teaser on page one that asked, "*Who's Funding the Gordon Campaign?*"

The Bijou once again took up most of the front page. **BIJOU SAVED**, the banner headline blared. Tall Rawls had scored an interview with Nadine, in which she shared her hope to resell the building to someone with a feasible plan for adaptive reuse.

"I should have grabbed Nadine Lattimore for the podcast yesterday instead of waiting a respectful period," Lynda rebuked herself, tossing that section of the paper over to me. "If she talked to Johanna about the building, she might have been willing to talk to me about the murder. I guess Johanna was too busy working on such a hot story to give me a heads-up."

She sounded a little hurt by her protégé's lapse. My mind was working in other directions. "When Oscar asked Nadine who benefited by her husband's death, she offered up Mac because of his Bijou-saving activism. Oscar didn't take that seriously, of course, but the fact that the Bijou isn't going to be torn down does create a motive for somebody."

"Like Brenda Thomas, for instance?"

"Who's that?"

"Check out the sidebar."

Another Tall Rawls story on page 4A, packaged with the jump from the front-page interview with the widow, profiled Ms. Thomas as a wedding planner with a business plan to create an event space at the Bijou if she could land state of Ohio tax credits available for historic renovation. "The building is certainly historic, and qualifies in every way," she asserted to the reporter. "I'm confident that we can secure this funding."

The "we" was apparently a royal or editorial "we," because no partner was mentioned. Ms. Thomas did drop the name of Serena Mason, however, saying that the philanthropist had been very supportive in trying to help her get the tax credits dished out by the Ohio Development Services Agency.

"This woman seems to be several important steps ahead of Saylor-Mackie and Kendric Armstrong," I noted when I'd finished reading the story. "They would like to get their hands on the Bijou for the SBU drama department, but Brenda Thomas actually has a plan to do it. That potentially makes her a major beneficiary of Davenport's death."

"But she only has a motive if she *knew* that Nadine would put the kibosh on the hotel plan after she inherited Davenport's businesses."

"True," I conceded. "The killer couldn't just assume that removing Davenport would eliminate the problem. That's an objection to suspecting any of the 'Save-the-Bijou' folks. We need to find out if anybody knew how Nadine felt about the demolition plan."

"One person did for sure."

"Who?"

Lynda picked Donata out of her high chair and set her on the floor, whereupon our girl immediately toddled off, as toddlers do.

"Nadine Lattimore, of course."

"You think she'd kill her husband just because she didn't like his business plan?"

Lynda shrugged. "Stranger things have happened. You know that. In real life, people are weird. But maybe axing the Bijou project was just part of something bigger— like getting control of all his businesses and his money. Or maybe she has a boyfriend. Jordan Webster is kind of cute."

"I wouldn't say that. His mouth is too big."

This was spinning rapidly out of control.

"I know a lot of people in Cincinnati television," Lynda reminded me. "I'll ask around, see if there's any gossip about Nadine. That would be rich material for the podcast—unless Grier and Channel Eleven's parent company become strategic partners, of course."

Of course.

"For the podcast!" Mac raised both eyebrows. "Is our investigation to become an aural reality show?"

"Forgive her. She's pregnant. But it did occur to me yesterday that Nadine could have been the person who visited Davenport in male disguise, knowing that the surveillance camera would pick her up. As a TV anchor, she's practically a professional actor."

"And she once aspired to be an opera singer." I could practically hear the gears turning in Mac's oversized head. "Irene Adler, an opera singer 'of dubious and questionable memory,' was known to don male attire on occasion as a disguise. Ingenious, Jefferson!"

I denied myself the pleasure of pointing out that Irene Adler was a fictional character in a Sherlock Holmes story. Although fun, that would have somewhat undercut my line of thought.

"And if Nadine *was* fooling around," I asserted, "Davenport wasn't the sort to just close his eyes to it. So, she would have had a strong motive, never mind that she seems very nice on camera and off. We've known nice killers before."

Discussing this over cappuccino (healthy for me, caffeinated for Mac) at the Beans & Books coffee house and used book store, we were soon joined by Oscar. Out of uniform, he had covered his balding dome with a shapeless canvas fishing hat. Lynda was back at the ranch, enjoying a mid-morning nap with our daughter. Beryl Peacock, our favorite server at B&B, brought Oscar a steaming mug of an oil-like substance before his substantial rump had even landed on the chair. We filled him in on our chats of the day before, ending with Lynda's speculations—and mine—about Nadine Lattimore.

"As it happens, something like that had occurred to yours truly." Oscar smiled and took his third gulp of caffeine. "So, I sent Gibbons to Channel Eleven to confirm Ms. Lattimore's alibi. Three of her co-workers are sure she arrived at the station at ten o'clock. Apparently, they pay attention to time in the TV news business. If she left the Lyceum at intermission, which was nine-fifteen, she must have had her foot to the pedal and no stops on the way to get there by that time. So, her alibi is solid at that end.

"But Gibbons, being Gibbons, didn't stop there. He ran down the Lyceum's parking lot attendant that night, one Scooter McBride. McBride recognized his favorite TV news anchor getting her car at intermission, just as she'd said. So that's that."

"How did Mr. McBride know it was intermission?" Mac inquired.

"Because she left the theater right along with all the smokers who were running out *en masse* to get their fixes." If Oscar spoke with a touch of smugness in his tone, it was because he doesn't consider vaping to be smoking.

Lynda should be recording this for the podcast, I thought. Since she wasn't, I made a mental note to suggest that she interview Gibbons about his routine but painstaking detective work. Audiences seem to love that stuff on TV shows.

"Of course," Oscar added, "if what we have here is a homicidal spouse, she could have gotten help from somebody—like a boyfriend, for instance."

"Lynda's looking into that," I informed him. "She's plugging into the local media gossip mill to see what tongues are wagging about. If there's fire, there must be some smoke."

"Not a bad idea. We're going to keep beating the bushes in the Davenports' neighborhood. Maybe somebody saw something. Meanwhile, with the widow's permission, I checked the calendar on Davenport's smartphone to verify that he had an appointment that night. It checks out. 'Pinkerton' is in the nine-thirty slot."

"A cynic would say that Nadine could have added that appointment herself," Mac noted.

"Only if she's really techno-smart. The phone was locked with TouchID technology. It took Davenport's thumbprint to unlock it."

Oscar obviously wanted us to ask, so I did. "Then how did you do it?"

"Most people don't know this, but with TouchID the thumb doesn't have to be attached to a living body as long as the owner of the thumb hasn't been dead more than forty-eight hours."

"Brilliant!" Mac declared.

"I saw it on *Midwest Murders* a few weeks back," the Chief admitted.

"You watch that program?" I said. I wouldn't go near it with a sleeping mask over my eyes and plugs in my ears, but Lynda loves it. It's one of those reality shows with often-painful attempts to create suspense with voice-overs as the story unfolds.

"Why not? I bet the bad guys do. It's very educational. They had a doozy on last week: A prosecutor up in Butler County used the GPS on a guy's phone to put him at the scene of the murder at the relevant time."

"*Midwest Murders* runs on Channel Eleven, Nadine's station," I mused. "It's on right before her newscast on Thursday nights. But I suppose she's normally too tied up right before air time to watch it."

"Did you happen to notice on the smartphone who else had appointments with Mr. Davenport in recent days?" Mac asked.

"There was no 'happen' about it, Sherlock. I looked for it." He consulted a small notebook tucked into his shirt pocket. "In the last month the victim had scheduled meetings with Lesley Saylor-Mackie, Sheila Paxton, his wife, Jordan Webster, Bruce Gordon, and Wade Pennington."

"He put his wife on his calendar?" I asked.

"Is that unusual?"

"I thought I was the only one."

"Was the meeting with Bruce Gordon before or after his change of position on the Bijou project?" Mac inquired.

"Two days before. Looks like one might have led to the other."

"I'm shocked, shocked," I said in my best Captain Renault voice from *Casablanca*.

"The only name on the calendar that stands out to me is Wade Pennington, since they weren't exactly buddies," Oscar said.

"On the surface, it does seem to be an anomaly," Mac said. "However, there is an explanation. Mr. Pennington mentioned that meeting to Jefferson and me." Mac related how the late developer, according to Pennington, had insulted the candy man on that occasion by suggesting that he could simply move his candy store. "Apparently it was something of a charm offensive on Hunter Davenport's part that came a cropper."

"Sounds plausible. Charm doesn't seem to have been his strong suit, but that doesn't mean he wouldn't give it a go." Oscar returned the notebook to his pocket. "What are you geniuses going to do next?"

"I am eager to speak with Ms. Thomas," Mac said.

"Who?"

"Don't you read the *Observer*?"

"Not today. I just got back from fishing. Which reminds me—" He picked up the hand-printed menu Beryl had deposited along with the coffee. "—I could eat a horse."

While Oscar made a pretense of scanning the menu before ordering his usual heart-attack on a plate, Mac filled him in on Brenda Thomas's plans for the Bijou building—plans which might move ahead now that Hunter Davenport was dead.

Oscar harrumphed. "Sounds like you're grasping at straws."

"Perhaps," Mac acknowledged. "At least we are grasping."

Chapter Thirteen
The Wedding Planner

Brenda Thomas worked as a wedding planner out of her home, a handsome red brick number in a neighborhood where all the lawns were nicely landscaped. A "Save the Bijou" yard sign decorated hers. Maybe she'd been too busy to remove it, or maybe keeping it up was a kind of triumphalism. I never got around to asking.

"As you might imagine, I am quite interested in your plans for the Bijou," Mac told her after she'd welcomed us into a charming French provincial living room that to my sensitive nose smelled strongly of tobacco smoke. A phone call had paved the way, with Mac introducing himself—unnecessarily, it turned out—as the leader of the resistance to Davenport Development's nefarious plans.

"Before we get into that, I want to say that I appreciate all you did to keep that gem of a building from being torn down." Brenda Thomas spoke briskly, with all the authority of a woman who spent much of her time battling Bridezillas. Probably over fifty, she was an attractive woman with platinum hair who even on a Saturday morning was turned out in a fetching gray dress set off by black onyx earrings and equally black high heels.

Mac waved aside the compliment with an airy hand. "Truth to tell, it was Hunter Davenport's death that saved the Bijou."

Nice segue into the real reason we're here!

The wedding planner frowned. "I was no fan of Davenport or the way he did business, but I certainly didn't want that to happen to him. His wife must be devastated. She seems pleasant enough on TV. Still, it's an ill wind that blows no good, as my grandmother used to say."

Granny may have been a wise woman, but she wasn't a very original one.

"What sparked your interest in turning the Bijou building into an events center?" Mac asked.

"The events center idea came first. Do you mind if I smoke, Mr. McCabe? It's a lousy habit for a runner, but I can't break it."

Hey, why don't you ask me? I mind!

Mac beamed. "Of course not. I enjoy cigars myself. And we have not yet come to the point where a person cannot indulge in a legal vice in her own home."

Brenda Thomas had a long cigarette ignited before Mac had begun his second sentence. I tried not to cough.

"I started out as a cake decorator more than thirty years ago and morphed into a wedding planner when the field started to gain traction," Thomas said between puffs. She didn't invite Mac to join her in this legal vice. Maybe she didn't like cigars. "Do you have any idea how limited the venues are for wedding receptions in Erin?"

"My wife and I ran into that problem five years ago," I offered. Almost exactly five years, it was—we had just celebrated our anniversary a little more than a week before.

Our hostess nodded. "Okay, you know what I mean, then. So, Erin could use an events center. It would be great for the city, and not incidentally great for me. I'd been thinking about that for a while when I noticed the Bijou building one day while I was running on Front Street. The building was a wreck, of course—but what potential! The space is very workable for all kinds of events, and especially receptions. Plus, the Bijou has a great story. It always helps to have a story. Imagine my shock when I found out that the building had been bought just a few months earlier by a developer who wanted to tear it down. I was devastated."

"But undaunted," Mac observed.

"When I get an idea, I'm not easily dissuaded. You don't think it's a piece of cake to set up as a wedding planner in a town this size, do you?"

Surprisingly, I'd never really thought about it.

Mac ignored the rhetorical question, even though he loves cake. "I gather from the story in the *Observer* that you went to Serena Mason for help with your idea."

"Right. I've known Serena for years. She's so good at giving money away that people forget she's also a shrewd businesswoman. She inherited her husband's family money, sure, but she made her own pile as well. A couple of weeks ago I tried to sign her on as a partner in my new venture, but she wasn't having any. Serena's fully committed to Serenity House now. She told me she even had to turn down a request to be season sponsor of the Erin Opera, although she's a big opera buff. But she did give me a good tip on the state tax credits."

Thomas's cell phone rang. She looked at the number. "Excuse me. Client calling."

She answered and began talking as she wandered into another room. "Hello, Beth . . ."

I had a comment ready for her when she returned:

"But after the Zoning Board of Appeals approval of the Bijou demolition, your idea was going nowhere while Davenport was alive."

"Don't be so sure." Thomas smiled. "You weren't going to throw in the towel, were you, Mr. McCabe?"

Mac grew an inch. "By no means."

"There you are! And I—"

Thomas was interrupted by the opening of the front door, followed by the appearance in the hallway of a millennial male with shaggy fair hair and a general air of having just rolled out of bed. He was dressed in a Beatles T-shirt and chinos.

"Oh, sorry, I didn't know you had company."

It took me a few seconds to place him out of context, but the attempted mustache did the trick. I'd seen him at the *Claudette* reception, where Tall Rawls had pointed him out to Lynda and me.

"This is my son, Manny Templeton," our hostess informed us with an indulgent smile just as I figured that out—his identity, not his relationship to Brenda Thomas. To him she said, "We were just talking about my vision for the Bijou building." She told Templeton who we were. We exchanged handshakes all around.

"Your name is not unknown to me," Mac told the newcomer. "Your effort to force City Council to follow the state sunshine law was rather big news until it was overshadowed by the Davenport murder."

"I'm proud of Manny," his mother said before he could respond. She looked it.

"No doubt."

"They think that just because this is a small town they can get by flouting the law, but I wasn't going to let them," Templeton said. "I'm kind of surprised the *Observer* printed what I told them. This town is full of scandals that rag won't touch." *Probably a good thing Lynda isn't here.* "I'm thinking of starting my own blog called 'The Scoop' to expose them. How do you like that name?"

"It sings," I assured him before Mac could comment. *Don't give up your day job.* But did he have a day job? I decided to find out with a subtle question: "If there's as much dirty-doings to report as you say, wouldn't a blog take up a lot of your time?"

"I'm a life coach. My hours are flexible."

My phone pinged to announce an incoming text, but I decided it could wait.

"Your crusade may be a noble one," Mac said, "and yet it hardly seems disinterested. A more open process at City Hall would have especially benefited those of us who opposed demolition of that fine old theater—including you, Ms. Thomas."

She smoked furiously. "I don't like your implication, Mr. McCabe."

Mac was all innocence. "You infer an implication? I merely stated a fact."

"I wasn't trying to help anybody," Templeton said. "My only interest is the civic good. Citizen-taxpayers have a right to know what our lawmakers are up to. The public business should be done in public. That's not only right, it's the law in Ohio, which a majority of City Council members have been flaunting."

"It was most admirable of you to call attention to that breach, Mr. Templeton. And presumably you are not the only civic-minded person in this business. Whoever informed you of Council members' infraction was no doubt of the same mind. I presume that anonymous hero was someone closer to the scene, perhaps a disgruntled City Hall functionary?"

Templeton's scanty mustache did sit-ups while he gave that a think.

"I'm not saying," he finally announced. *No surprise there.* "It doesn't matter how I found out, anyway. You talked about stating a fact. Five City Council members violated the law. That's a fact."

"Touché! That I must concede. However, the identity of your informant is of great interest to me nonetheless."

"Why?" Brenda Thomas demanded.

Mac apparently decided to put his cards on the table—or, at least, some of them. "Perhaps you are aware that from time to time I have dabbled in helping Chief Hummel and other law enforcement officials to solve murders when standard police methods have proved fruitless. It is in that context that your son's revelation intrigues me. It seems obvious to me that blowing that particular whistle at this particular time was not done by someone who wished the late Hunter Davenport well."

"You mean Manny's informant might be a good suspect for the murder." Brenda Thomas lit her third cigarette off her second.

"Conceivably."

"No way," her son said.

But that's all he would say.

Chapter Fourteen
Dark Money

Outside the house, I checked the text that had come in while Mac and Templeton were dueling. It was from Lynda. *Meet me at the Observer pronto. Bring Mac.*

She had maintained an office at the newspaper even after moving up the Grier corporate food chain, but there was no need for us to look for her there. She waylaid us at the front door. "Fortesque walked in with a story, and Ben thought I might be interested in it for the podcast."

Away from his houseboat, Reginald "Scrappy Smith" Fortesque still dressed nautically in his yachting cap. His feet, encased in those pricey deck shoes, were put up on the big table of the *Observer* conference room. He should have had a martini in his hand.

"Hello, boys," he said cheerfully upon our entrance. "Do you want to join my complaint?"

"What complaint is that?" Mac asked.

"On Monday morning, Mr. Fortesque plans to file a grievance with the Erin Elections Commission against Bruce Gordon for taking campaign contributions from all those LLCs," Ben Silverstein filled us in. No slouch of a dresser himself, Ben sat across the table from Fortesque with his vest carefully buttoned.

"I thought that was legal," I objected.

"Maybe it is and maybe it isn't," the candidate said. "Suppose he took the maximum contribution of eleven hundred dollars from an individual, and then took multiples of that from the same individual hiding behind all those LLCs? Wouldn't that push the individual's contribution over the limit? The campaign finance reports don't say who controls those entities. Maybe my complaint will force Gordy to say. Know what I think? I think most of the money came from Davenport." *You're not alone there, Scrappy!* "He bribed Gordy to change his position on the Bijou project because it looked like Gordy could be the deciding vote if it came down to Council. What are you doing?"

This last was said to Lynda.

"Taping you for my podcast. This is strong stuff."

"It's about to get stronger. I say Gordy could have killed Davenport to hide their dirty dealings. I wouldn't put it past him."

Mac stroked his beard thoughtfully. "No, Reginald, as attractive as that idea might be, it will not wash. Whether the contributions were legal or not, they were reported. And the LLC addresses led right back to the generous Mr. Davenport. Killing him would not have concealed that."

"But only Hunter Davenport and Bruce Gordon could say for sure what caused Gordy to change his vote, and now one of them is dead. The buying and selling of votes is illegal under both federal and state law, although hard to establish. Gordy could do serious prison time if Davenport turned against him and could prove their deal."

"Davenport might have had some evidence, if that really happened," Ben said, "but I don't suppose you do."

"Not yet. I'm counting on Gordy to panic and do something stupid."

Ben scribbled away in a small notebook.

"Hey, don't print that." The former homeless man took his feet off the table. "I don't want to warn Gordy off."

"Technically, it's too late to go off the record after you say something," Ben informed him. He closed the notebook. "I won't use it, though. It seems a bit reckless for you to accuse a political opponent of murder."

"But I have it on tape for later in case Gordon really does turn out to be the killer," Lynda said.

"Feel free," Scrappy told her. I always thought of him as "Scrappy" when he was at his feistiest, which was most of the time.

"Oscar is proceeding on the assumption that the person who had an appointment with Mr. Davenport that night under the alias of Pinkerton was the killer," Mac related. "The pseudonymous Pinkerton appears on the surveillance video of the Davenport home. His figure is, shall we say, not as broad as that of Bruce Gordon."

Or of Sebastian McCabe.

Scrappy shrugged. "Don't video cameras make people look thinner?"

"No, fatter," my doubly pregnant wife snapped.

"How come you didn't report any campaign contributions?" I asked. "Don't you have any supporters wanting to fund your run?"

"Hundreds," Scrappy said. "I turned them all down. I'm paying for this crusade with my own money. I'm all in. If I don't invest in Fortesque for Mayor, how can I ask anybody else to do it? This is going to be the best money I ever spent."

Bruce Gordon's list of character flaws would fill a reporter's notebook, but laziness isn't one of them. We found him at his shop, still selling flowers at five o'clock on that Saturday afternoon.

"Ah, now comes the press!" he said, addressing Ben and Lynda with a forced smile. "And Sebastian McCabe, our local super-sleuth." He didn't acknowledge me, for which I was just as glad. "Something tells me you aren't here to buy roses."

By pre-agreement, Ben took the lead. "You didn't return my phone calls asking for comment on the story about your campaign financing."

"I've been busy. I've a got a small business to run here. I'm not independently wealthy like my two opponents."

"Do you mind if I record this conversation?" Lynda asked, holding up her device.

"Why the hell should I mind? If I say it, I mean it. Record anything you want, and use it any way you want. What do you think I am, a politician?"

Vote the Rascal in!

"Ms. Teal and I would rather ask questions than answer them, if you don't mind," Ben said mildly. "We have just come from an interview with one of your electoral rivals, Reginald Fortesque."

"Fortesque! I remember when he was known as Scrappy Smith, living on the streets. And he was a millionaire the whole time! The man's a nutball."

The words *pot, kettle,* and *black* occurred to me.

"That may or may not be," Ben said, "but your opponent has made a very serious charge against you—a couple of them, really. First, he alleges that the multiple LLCs that contributed thousands of dollars to your campaign were all controlled by Hunter Davenport, who also gave the maximum amount under his own name."

"Yeah, that's true. So what?"

Lynda almost dropped the digital recorder. "You admit it?"

"I don't *admit* a damned thing. I *acknowledge* that Hunter was my biggest supporter. 'Admit' is what a man does when he's guilty of something."

"Mr. Fortesque told us he plans to file a complaint against your campaign with the Erin Elections Commission. He's going to argue that the combined contributions funneled to the campaign through numerous Limited

Liability Companies exceed the dollar limit under Ohio law because in reality they come from the same person."

Bruce Gordon smiled like a movie villain. "Good luck with that. The Elections Commission decided eight years ago, during my first Council campaign, that a civic-minded man, woman, or child can make contributions as an individual and also through an LLC or several LLCs. And the Commission further ruled that the contribution limit only applies to each separate contribution, not to all of them in the aggregate."

"I suspect that you have good reason to remember that ruling," Mac said, unable to restrain himself any longer.

"Sure do. I filed the complaint against one of the other Council candidates that resulted in that ruling. Obviously, I lost."

"If this is all above board, why didn't you identify Davenport as the man behind the LLCs in your finance report?" Lynda asked.

"I just didn't think of it. If it'll make my esteemed opponent happy, I'll amend my filing first thing Monday morning. You can watch me do it, take some photos for the paper. How does that sound?"

I had to mentally hand it to the old fox for turning a controversy into a positive photo op. By Monday morning, as it turned out, the *Observer* and Lynda would have a lot bigger story than a candidate's photo op to deal with.

Before the journalists could respond to Gordy's suggestion, the cell phone in his pocket burst into "You Are My Sunshine." The perpetually pugnacious look on his face softened.

"Just a minute."

He turned away from us and spoke softly into the phone. "Hi, honey." I heard a female voice on the other end. "Okay. I'll be home soon. I promise." He kissed the phone, then disconnected and slipped it back into his pocket. "My wife is having a bad day. Reaction to chemo."

I never know how to respond to comments like that, so I didn't. None of us did.

"I'd better take her orchids," Gordy muttered to himself.

Mac cleared his throat. "Perhaps we had better take our leave after Mr. Silverstein addresses the most serious charge your opponent leveled."

"What now?"

Ben looked embarrassed. "I do need to ask you about that. Fortesque alleges that you changed your position on the Bijou development to one of support because of those large campaign contributions from Davenport. He even suggests you could have killed Davenport to cover up your crime."

Just because Ben didn't plan to use the charge, that didn't mean he couldn't ask about it.

If Gordy wasn't stunned, he gave a good impression of it. "What? Me kill Davenport? That's crazy even for Scrappy Smith. And what crime was I supposed to have committed?"

"Selling your vote for campaign contributions, of course," Lynda said.

"What vote?"

Light dawned in the deep brown eyes of Sebastian McCabe. "There was no vote!"

"That's right. The issue hasn't come before City Council and now it looks like it never will. The project is as dead as Davenport."

Gordy's supposed motive was melting like an ice cream cone in Phoenix in July.

He waved the whole thing away. "But no matter, you've got it all wrong. I didn't change my position because of Davenport's support. It was the other way around. I got his support because I changed my position."

"The timeline hardly supports that," Mac pointed out. "The campaign money flowed to you only after you reversed your stance on the Bijou demolition."

"It only looks like that. I told Davenport during a private meeting about my change of heart a couple of days before I announced it. That's when he decided to contribute to my campaign. It was just a matter of logistics that the money didn't actually flow into my campaign coffers until after the Conservation Board hearing."

"Did anybody else hear your conversation with Davenport about this?" Ben asked.

"No. That's what 'private' means. You're not actually thinking of publishing that outrageous speculation, are you? It's not only libelous, it's ridiculous! I had no reason to kill Davenport. Plus, I was at the opera that night. Most of you saw me there! Unless you think I hired a hit man?"

"The prospect of finding a professional assassin in Erin does seem rather remote," Mac allowed.

But Lynda had a notion. "There's a lot of nastiness in the world today, and nowhere more so than in politics. Do you think somebody might have killed your biggest campaign contributor to hurt your campaign?"

Gordy looked at her for a minute, the expression on his face indicating that he was counting her heads.

"It's a little late for that, don't you think, Ms. Teal? The election is still a long way off, but I've already raised more money than Lesley Saylor-Mackie in either of her campaigns for mayor. And she won big both times. I already have this election in the bag."

Chapter Fifteen
Backstage Murder

"So, what do we have?" Lynda asked as we assembled in Mac's man cave on Sunday afternoon after Mass. Kate was at the Lyceum for the fourth and final performance of *Claudette,* and two of the three McCabe kids were playing with Donata downstairs in the basement family room.

"We have a mess," I opined.

"Hardly that," Mac demurred, ensconced in his overstuffed chair as if it were a throne. He seemed content to let me play master of ceremonies. Or maybe ringmaster. Which I did:

"I beg to differ. Let's start with Lynda's favorite candidate, Nadine Lattimore. You're on, Lyn. Tell him what you found out."

She made a face that had chagrin written all over it, but was still pretty. "Everybody in the TV news business in Chicago and in the Queen City loves her and nobody thinks she's fooling around. And if it isn't being gossiped about, it for sure hasn't happened. I guess I shouldn't feel so disappointed at finding out that a nice person is also a good person, but I can't help it."

"Throw in the alibi and I think we can count her out," I said, "even though she inherits a bundle. As you pointed out, Mac, hired killers are not a dime a dozen in Erin."

"I bet they are in Chicago," Lynda put in with a hopeful lilt in her voice.

"Nobody who makes her living in front of a camera would put herself under the thumb of a hit man, my dear. Let's move on. Bruce Gordon also has an alibi and a belly too big to be the guy, or the woman, on the surveillance tape. And he has a distinct lack of motive, so far as we know. All that fancy footwork over campaign contributions might sell a few papers—"

"Let's hope so," Lynda murmured. She squirmed, uncomfortable with the bulk of the two new Codys in utero.

"—but nobody would kill for it, not even a screwball like Gordy," I said. "What's wrong with his wife, by the way? She's doing chemo."

"Polly said Louise LaRosa told her that Betty Gordon has breast cancer, but the prognosis is good. Keep her in your prayers."

After a promise to do so and a respectful pause, I went on: "Speaking of screwballs, we have to put Reginald Fortesque III and Lani Alvarez on the suspect list just so we can cross them off. As Gordy pointed out, Davenport had already turned on the money machine, so killing him didn't affect that."

"What about revenge for what he had done, not preventing him from doing something in the future?" Lynda said.

"Although both other mayoral candidates have spent time as guests of Oscar's jail, neither has a record of violence," Mac said. "That is not to say that they are incapable of it, given the right circumstances. Retribution for a series of questionable political contributions hardly qualifies as the right circumstance, however. Still, the revenge motif has its attraction. The Holmes Canon is full of revenge killers."

"Sherlock isn't here," Lynda reminded him, "and we're counting on you to fill the void. What about the other suspects?"

"Let's start with Sheila Paxton," I said. "You recorded her for the podcast, Lyn. Nadine Lattimore was reluctant to mention her name anywhere near the word 'suspect.' She obviously likes Sheila."

"It's hard not to," Lynda said. "She has the drive and the self-confidence of a winner, without the arrogance."

"Well said," Mac agreed. "And her assertion of gratitude for Davenport's investment in her dream seemed genuine. However, she does gain financially by his death."

"Not as much as his wife does." That was Lynda, of course.

"Still, *cui bono* is never to be ignored, although I am inclined to think that Ms. Paxton's highly entrepreneurial mind runs in directions other than homicide."

"So, we don't cross her off," Lynda said, "but we don't think she's a great suspect. Well, how about that mother-son team?"

"Manny Templeton's pretense that he's a disinterested civic gadfly is laughable," I said. "He lives at home. He's clearly fighting City Hall to help his mother—who, by the way, is one tough cookie. I'd bet on her over any Bridezilla." *But not over my mother-in-law.* I shuddered at the thought of Lynda's mom and her wedding antics. "You should grab her for the podcast. She could be a lively postscript on the future of the Bijou, if nothing else."

"The death of Hunter Davenport does clear the way for Brenda Thomas to realize her vision of turning the Bijou building into an events center," Mac said. "However, there are many other steps along the way and ultimate success is by no means a certainty. Even if she somehow knew that Ms. Lattimore would jettison the development plan upon her husband's death—a dubious possibility—there was no certainty that Ms. Thomas could acquire the building, secure the state tax credits, and get a loan. Homicide seems like a bridge too far in the face of all of that. Risk is part of the entrepreneurial DNA, but I would suggest that murder is too much risk for too little gain in this instance, just as with Ms. Paxton."

"I suppose it's not fair to say the killer may be crazy."

"No, old boy, I am afraid not. That would not be playing the game."

"We're almost through the whole list of suspects, scraping the bottom of the barrel. Dr. Hawthorne used to own the Bijou building—or rather, his wife did. I think he's just glad he got a little money out of it and didn't get dragged into the controversy. I don't even remember why we talked to him."

"Wade Pennington supplied his name," Mac reminded me.

"Oh, yeah—the candy man. Why was he so eager to load us up with the names of potential suspects?"

"We asked, Jefferson."

"Well, he didn't have to answer. You saw how passionate Pennington was about Davenport at the Conservation Board hearing. Maybe he was twelve stabs' worth of passionate. He could have been unhinged by the disappointing turn of events, thinking the hotel project was scuttled and then finding out that the Zoning Board of Appeals had overturned that."

"Not bad," Lynda judged. "Could he be the person in the surveillance video?"

"That's marginal, I guess. We haven't seen it, but Oscar described Davenport's unknown visitor as 'slender, or at least not heavy.' Pennington is no tongue depressor, but he looks like he's lost a lot of weight recently. He still has the broad face of a bigger man."

Lynda sighed. "This is a mess."

I've been married long enough not to say, "I told you so." I was trying to figure out what I *should* say when Mac's phone rang. His ringtone sounds like—of all things—a telephone.

"Hello, Kate." Seldom have I seen a look of utter shock occupy the hairy mug of Sebastian McCabe, but it happened then. "We shall be right there. Thank you for calling." He disconnected.

"What?" Lynda almost yelled.

"Jordan Webster has been murdered. His body was found backstage at the Lyceum after the final curtain went down on *Claudette*."

ACT TWO

Chapter Sixteen
Not Everybody Loves Opera

The Lyceum Theater, a Victorian-era brick building that had been an Odd Fellows Hall for more than a century and a half, was already surrounded by yellow crime scene tape when we arrived. We nodded at the young officer standing guard, blithely ignored the barrier, and went on in.

On the stage, which was decorated for the Mardi Gras party in the final scene of the opera, stood several familiar figures and others I didn't recognize—the dozen or more non-performers, like the house manager and backstage assistant, that make an opera work.

Oscar was there, of course, with Lt. Col. L. Jack Gibbons in his party-goer costume as a supernumerary, along with Kate, Nadine Lattimore, assorted singers still dressed for their roles, and—

"Jordan Webster!" Mac exclaimed, just about the time my brain processed the identity of the figure in glasses and a blue turtleneck standing next to Nadine Lattimore. "By all that is holy, what has happened?"

In less than a minute we were up on the stage ourselves. Kate hugged Mac tightly, which is no easy task given his girth. If he were a lady, the opera wouldn't be over until he sang.

"It seems the reports of your death are greatly exaggerated," Mac told Webster. I made a mental note to complain to him later about the cliché.

"Sorry, Sebastian," Kate said. "We just found out. I was too discombobulated to send you an update."

"There was a mix-up," the young impresario said. "I feel terrible that somebody died instead of me."

"It's not your fault," Nadine assured him.

"Yes, it is."

His primary patron's widow patted Webster on the shoulder in a motherly way, although she was only a decade or so older. The Cody memory banks recalled her saying that she planned to catch the second act of *Claudette* that she'd missed on opening night. She was dressed for it casually in yellow slacks and a light pashmina in various subtle colors, probably with a designer label inside.

"Who was the victim?" Lynda asked.

Oscar jumped in, trying to maintain some semblance of control. "A teacher at Malcolm C. Cotton High named Aaron Schiff. He was a volunteer stagehand who took a turn today as an extra." *That's supernumerary in opera lingo.*

"I only knew him to nod to, but he seemed like a nice guy," Kate said. It wasn't much of a eulogy, but it was all she had. There was a respectful pause.

"When a costume designer found the body," Oscar resumed, "he thought it was Mr. Webster here."

We learned later that the unlucky fellow was Chase McAllister, a jeweler with a 20-year background of creating costumes for regional theater. Kate had worked backstage under his direction.

"Aaron was dressed in the Mardi Gras regalia I wore in all the other performances," Webster said miserably. "He practically begged me during intermission to let him go on stage during the final scene. I thought, why not? I said he could take my place and I would start working on some of the thousand things that have to be done behind the scenes at the end of an opera's run. He was about my size, so I just handed him my costume. That's why Chase didn't know."

"You were a supernumerary?" I said. I had visions of Alfred Hitchcock's famous habit of appearing for a few seconds in each of his films.

Webster nodded. "As artistic director, I wouldn't even need to be here, but I like to be on the scene during performances."

"And you don't sing?"

"My voice isn't of operatic quality."

"Jordan doesn't meet his own high standards," Nadine interpreted.

"Nor am I a talented conductor. That's why I brought in Maestro Kroskof."

He nodded toward the old man, who was still dressed in tails.

"Yes, you hired me to conduct!" I won't attempt to convey the Polish accent. Kroskof was in a tizzy, his face almost as white as his hair. "Why do you not let me conduct!" It wasn't a question, and he didn't wait for an answer. "Never have I been treated like this since I left Krakow fifty years ago! I will never work with you again, young man!"

Apparently, they had had artistic differences.

"Somebody killed this Schiff while he was dressed in the costume Webster wore in the other three performances of the opera," Oscar reminded us. "It's almost a sure bet that whoever stabbed him thought it was Webster he was skewering."

"Stabbed!" Mac repeated.

"Oh, yeah. We don't have a count yet, but there were multiple wounds. The killer took the weapon with him. Just like Davenport all the way. We're dealing with a repeat offender, no question."

"That changes everything," Mac said.

"Damn right it does," the Chief agreed gloomily. "The citizenry will be in a near-panic, convinced that a crazed serial killer is on the loose."

Lynda stuck the digital recorder in his face. She'd alerted Tall Rawls, who was on her way to cover the story for the *Observer*, but Lynda had a podcast to feed. "Tell us exactly what happened, Chief."

Oscar cleared his throat as I sent him a mental message: *Try not to use the word "pincushion."*

"Sometime during or just before the second and final act of *Claudette*, someone stabbed to death an extra named Aaron Schiff. The body, wearing a costume and mask, was found backstage in an out-of-the way passage shortly after the performance. Jordan Webster, the founder and artistic director of the Erin Opera Company, had seen the victim and talked with him during intermission, so we know he was alive then and he was dead shortly after the opera was over."

"Wasn't he missed during the performance?"

"Yes and no. He should have been among the revelers during the Mardi Gras party in the second act, which he wasn't, but it wasn't a singing part. His absence didn't constitute a crisis."

"And nobody saw what happened?"

"Our interviews are ongoing, but the picture that has emerged so far is one of normal chaos, what you would expect backstage at any theater. Apparently, a lot of the singers ran around dealing with wardrobe malfunctions or simply changing costumes from the previous act. Nobody was paying much attention to anybody else. A couple of them said they were 'in character,' whatever that means."

"It means that in their heads they were the characters they were portraying, not just actors playing parts," Webster informed us.

"If you say so."

"Interesting," Mac pronounced. "I had not considered that opera singers would be method actors."

The expression on Lynda's face suggested disapproval of this sidebar. It was of no use for her podcast.

"Anyway," Oscar resumed, "that's what we're getting so far from both cast and crew—even Gibbons. You'd think that with my best man on the scene during the murder . . ." Catching the eye of his assistant chief, who was still dressed like a court jester and blushing to the roots of his military-cut hair, Oscar mercifully dropped that line of thought. He recapped, in more formal language for the podcast, his near-certainty that Webster was the intended target.

"With all that bedlam behind the curtain," he added, "it's not impossible that someone unconnected with the opera could have snuck in unnoticed. Given that people trying to get into the opera without paying was not expected to be a big problem, security at the doors was lax."

"That won't happen again," Jordan declared, slamming that particular barn door.

Lynda turned her attention, and her digital recorder, toward him. "How does it feel to know that somebody tried to kill you?"

The answer was blunt and not slow in coming.

"Horrible."

"Couldn't some lunatic have attacked the victim because he didn't like the costume, not because of who was supposed to be wearing it?" I asked.

"I wish I could believe that," Webster said, "but a lot of people would have associated that costume with me. There was even a photo of me wearing it on the front page of the *Observer*."

Back to Oscar:

"What about that, Chief?" Lynda asked.

"Nothing has been ruled in or out at this stage, but the most probable scenario, as I indicated earlier, is that Mr. Webster was the intended target of the homicide."

"And neither access to the victim nor the expectation that Jordan Webster was the man behind the mask was limited to the cast and crew of *Claudette*," Mac thought out loud.

Tell me something I don't know.

Mac turned on Webster. "Please excuse the trite inquiry, but we would be remiss not to ask who might want to kill you."

"I don't know who, but it must be somebody who wants to sink the Erin Opera Company."

Mac raised an eyebrow.

"How do you figure that?" Oscar asked.

"From what you said, the same person who killed Hunter tried to kill me. What did the two of us have in common? The opera! Hunter sponsored the season, a fifty-thousand-dollar donation. I expected him to do the same again next year, and I needed him to. Even with volunteers and grants, we're barely making it. That's why we put up our singers in private homes." One of them, the actress who sang the title role of Claudette, was staying with Mac and Kate. "The killer had no way to know that Nadine would offer the same generous support." The look he gave her was one of gratitude, maybe with a splash of what Mac might call filial affection.

"That was a no-brainer on my part," Nadine said.

"Which was quickly reported in the *Observer*," Mac said, "making it clear that Mr. Davenport's death would not be fatal to the opera company."

A door closed at the back of the theater and Johanna Rawls nearly ran up the center aisle.

"I was in the shower when you called," she told Lynda, out of breath.

"Not another journalist!" Oscar exclaimed.

"It's just a matter of time before the AP gets here," I reminded him.

"Wonderful."

"I'll fill you in later," my spouse assured Johanna. "I have some sound you can use. May I see the poor man's body, Oscar?"

"The body is otherwise occupied and will soon be removed by the coroner's office."

"I was hoping to get a close-up look at the costume so I could describe it for the podcast."

"He was dressed in a top hat and black tailcoat to represent Baron Samedi, the voodoo spirit," my sister Kate said, speaking for the first time. "The skull mask covered his whole face. I added some shadows to it to highlight the effect."

"Too bad for Schiff the mask was so concealing," Oscar said. He sounded almost accusatory.

"Most Mardi Gras masks are," Kate volleyed back.

The climax of *Claudette* takes place at a Fat Tuesday ball, eighteen years after the dramatic conclusion of Act One. The now-fat and wealthy Jean-Christophe de Lubac, married but known to be a philanderer, falls under the spell of the mysterious Claudette Proulx. He sings in an aria that her beauty and her teasing drive him mad. And there is something familiar about her. (Anybody with an exposure to grand opera beyond a certain Bugs Bunny cartoon knows where this is going.)

De Lubac agrees to rendezvous with the mysterious woman at the masked ball. As he dons his costume he sings about the coincidence of what happened on this very night eighteen years ago, and how he is the only one left alive who knows the full story, having dealt with his henchmen long ago. Oh, if only Monique could have loved him instead of that pirate, may he rot in hell! Immediately after his last high note, Claudette—in her room which is shown at the other end of the stage—sings her own aria about the sweetness of revenge served cold.

At the ball, with the other masked guests acting as a kind of Greek chorus egging her on, Claudette rips off de

Lubac's mask and denounces him. He is her father, she sings—the rapist who is responsible for her dead mother's short life of sorrow! He has been playing the fool with his own daughter. She stabs him, then herself, dying happy in the arms of Jean Le Blanc, a young man she now learns has worshipped her from afar. Her mother and Pierre Remaux have been avenged and her life's purpose has been fulfilled. Young Le Blanc, not so happy, sings the last few lines: "Oh, my love! If only you had known my love, and I yours!"

I may have missed a murder here and a seduction there, but that was the gist of it. Mac proclaimed the opera "very Greek." Luther Kressel made it all up, except that there apparently was a real pirate known as Pierre Remaux (although his real name was McCullough and he was born and reared in Scotland).

"Look for a killer without a sense of drama," Lynda said. "The murder could have taken place right on stage and who would have noticed?"

"And it would have been excellent podcast material," Mac added, looking amused. "However, perhaps it is not a sense of drama the murderer lacks but the spirit of foolhardiness that would be required to take such a risk. Or perhaps he or she was simply not on the stage."

"And, therefore, could have been anybody—cast, crew, or somebody off the street," I said. "I think we already covered that."

Anybody meant anybody, from costumer Chase McAllister, only pretending to find the body, to supernumeraries like Kendric Armstrong. Well, not *any*body. I exempted Kate and Lt. Col. L. Jack Gibbons as being unthinkable on the face of it, not to mention having no motive that I could imagine. And I have a good imagination.

"If opportunity is so unhelpful in narrowing down our field of suspects, we had best turn our attention to motive," Mac said. "Why would anyone want to scuttle the Erin Opera Company, Mr. Webster?"

He shrugged his shoulders, the picture of dejection. "I can't imagine. Maybe some crazy opera-hater?"

Wait a minute! You rejected the lunatic theory when I proposed it.

"That seems a little far-fetched," Kate said, "but there have been protests against *Claudette*."

"Ah, yes, that would be the work of Ms. Alvarez, no stranger to my jail," Oscar said. "But killing two people, and one of them during the final performance of the opera, would be too drastic even for her. Not to mention pointless. This opera is home-grown stuff and may never even be performed again."

"Especially not after having two murders associated with it," I said. Then I had a brainstorm: "Maybe that was the idea—to establish the opera as cursed so it never gets put on again!"

"Ingenious, old boy!" Mac said. "I never get your limits. However, I feel constrained to point out that one of Shakespeare's plays has such a reputation for being cursed that actors dare not speak its name. Instead, they invariably use the euphemism 'The Scottish Play.' And yet it is still widely performed."

"But *Macb*—"

"Don't say that name in a theater, Jeff," my big sister interrupted loudly.

"This whole thing is demonic," Nadine Lattimore said with a fire in her wide green eyes. "Whether somebody wants to kill Jordan or destroy the opera company, it amounts to the same thing. The Erin Opera Company is his life."

"Well, maybe not exactly my life," the artistic director clarified, "but it is my passion."

"That could be significant to the motive," Mac said. "Animus toward you or your enterprise could even be the reason Hunter Davenport was killed, since his sponsorship was so crucial to the opera company. But if the murderer's intention is to harm you, Mr. Webster, and you were the direct target of the second murder, then the first would seem to be—pardon the word—overkill. Why not just start by killing you?"

Nadine looked stricken at the whole chain of reasoning. "That would be even more horrible, if someone killed Hunter to get at Jordan or to hurt the opera. I have no words."

"I can't make sense of any of it," Webster said. "All I know is that somebody tried to kill me and I'm sure still does. Do you think they'll just give up when they find out they made a mistake?"

His voice rose, both in pitch and in decibel level.

"I'll be honest," Oscar said, "I can't assign an officer to be your personal bodyguard for protection. But I'll have a cruiser drive by your house every few hours, looking for any suspicious activity."

Jordan didn't look very comforted, but the patrol eventually paid off.

Chapter Seventeen
The Art of Misdirection?

"At the risk of redundantly repeating myself," I said, "who would want to ring down the curtain on the Erin Opera Company?"

Not a bad line! I made a mental note to use it again.

The Codys and the McCabes, sharing a table at Bobbie McGee's Sports Bar that evening, were going over the events of the past week. By agreement, Lynda's digital recorder was hibernating

"Certainly not Lafcadio Figg," Kate said. Mac's old frenemy had showed up at the theater shortly after us in a panic, worried about the bad publicity attendant to murder at the Lyceum[5].

"Oh, I don't know," Lynda said. "In a *Scooby-Doo* plot, the killer would be the landlord who wants to get rid of the opera because he has a better tenant."

"And he would have gotten away with it, too," I added, "if it hadn't been for those meddling kids. They would have ripped off his mask in the final scene."

"There is at least one masquerade in this affair other than Aaron Schiff's," Mac mused. "Surely the person called Pinkerton was in disguise. However, I can conceive of no better tenant for Lafcadio than the Erin Opera Company with its two annual productions. In addition, the Lyceum

---

[5] He should have been used to it. The first production of the Lyceum Players was marred by a murder behind the theater in the year of our wedding. See *The 1895 Murder*, MX Publishing, 2012.

will face new competition if the Bijou, no longer threatened with extinction by Hunter Davenport, is revived as a theater for St. Benignus, as the Provost and Kendric Armstrong have bandied about. The Davenport murder, therefore, was not in Lafcadio's best interest."

"Figg probably didn't know that Nadine would pull the plug on the hotel project," I pointed out.

"Most likely not, I concede. Still, I must reluctantly agree that Lafcadio is perhaps the least likely suspect."

And therefore guilty!

"Then why hasn't he begged you to solve the murders, the way he did in that QueenCon business last year?"[6]

"Perhaps because he realizes that I need no such prompting to take a hand, Jefferson. Whatever his deficiencies, Lafcadio is not a dolt."

"Well, the killer isn't Nadine Lattimore, either," Lynda opined. "She's too fond of opera *and* of Jordan Webster, not to mention her husband."

"Do you believe that she is enamored of Mr. Webster?" Mac asked.

She shook her head, sending her honey-colored curls bouncing. "Not the way you mean. If I read her body language right, it's more like he's the son she never had, although he's a little old for the role." I'd been thinking along the same lines. "Plus, she's really into this whole opera thing—which is another reason it makes no sense that she would have killed a man she believed was Jordan Webster. I think she wants to be his Catherine de' Medici, his patron."

"You've really done a one-eighty on Nadine as a suspect," I noted.

"I'm just going where the facts take me, like I always tell reporters to do. So, she's 'Nadine,' is she?"

---

[6] See *Queen City Corpse* (MX Publishing, 2017).

She was just kidding, I'm sure.

"What about Grayson Caldwell?" I offered.

Mac looked intrigued. "Elaborate, Jefferson."

"I just remembered that his review of *Claudette* took potshots at the Erin Opera Company. Why would a big-name maven take the trouble to attend a small-town opera and then trash the effort?"

"Maybe because he's a jerk," Lynda suggested.

"Everybody's a critic," I quipped.

Mac moved on.

"Dr. Hawthorne went out of his way to say he loves opera," he mused. "Perhaps that was a charade to conceal just the opposite."

"I think you've been reading too many of your own books, Sebastian," Kate said. "David hasn't missed a season of the Cincinnati Opera in something like fifteen years. We've seen him there with Rosalie several times, remember? And I know from her that she didn't drag him there." Kate and Rosalie Gamble Hawthorne have been friends for years.

If it were possible for Mac to look humbled, he would have.

"And anyway," Kate rolled on, "as you said earlier, why would anybody take such a roundabout way to hurt the opera? Killing Jordan is all it would take. He's the heart and soul of it. Maybe the opera company is his life, as Nadine Lattimore said, but it also works the other way—he's the life of the opera company."

"But maybe the killer didn't realize that," I said. "It wouldn't be obvious to somebody who wasn't close to the situation."

"Sebastian, you're going to have to solve these murders and save the opera," Kate said.

Is that all?

Mac sighed, a sound reminiscent of a water buffalo in heat. "Our investigation into the Davenport murder up to now was based on an apparently false premise that led us down the garden path. It would seem that the Bijou drama, for all its sound and fury, had nothing to do with Mr. Davenport's demise."

"Or maybe it did!" Lynda's gold-flecked brown eyes flashed. "Maybe the second murder is just a smokescreen to make the motive of the first murder less obvious."

Mac fiddled with his beard, either pondering or pretending. "In the parlance of the stage magician, that would be called misdirection. The technique certainly has a long and distinguished pedigree in detective fiction."

"Yeah, I know—Agatha Christie." Lynda named one of her novels involving multiple murders, with all but one of them window dressing. If you don't know which one, I'm not telling you. "And 'The Murdoch Mysteries' used the same idea in the sixth season."

"If it's good enough for Murdoch—" I stopped, struck by a brainstorm. "What a minute! Maybe *Davenport's* murder was the red herring, not Aaron Schiff's. In the Christie book, the real victim wasn't the first one killed. And come to that, maybe Aaron Schiff was the intended target all along!" I had quite a head of steam going.

"But who would want to kill him?" Kate asked.

"How should I know? That's Mac's job."

"The possibility certainly bears investigation," my brother-in-law allowed, "even though it seems almost too Golden Age to be true."

"This is all brilliant," Lynda said. "I wish I hadn't agreed not to record it."

"If any of this turns out to be true, you can reconstruct it," I said.

She gave me a withering stare reminiscent of her mother on those rare occasions when the latter was not being seductive. *What did I say?* Hey, so-called "reality TV" fakes stuff all the time, even those house-hunting shows.

"Hello there!"

The cheerful voice invading our table space belonged to Mac and Kate's houseguest, Tiffany Carmichael, who was bunked down in my old apartment above the McCabe garage. A soprano and former classmate of Webster's from Racine, Wisconsin, she normally sang in cabarets in Cologne, Germany.

We greeted her with handshakes all round. She hadn't been in town long enough to reach the hugging stage. But I knew her well enough to know that she was no prima donna, as the term is usually used, even though she technically *was* a prima donna.

"I still can't believe what happened today," Tiffany bubbled as she pulled up an empty chair to make herself at home. She was about five-six, slim, with short blond hair that she covered with a waist-long, dark wig while singing the part of Claudette. She smelled of lavender. "That pudgy police chief asked us all to not leave town, just like in a movie. This should get more publicity than any opera I've been in." *It's an ill-wind* . . . "Too bad it's the wrong kind!"

"Not all the publicity was bad," Lynda pointed out. "Grayson Caldwell reviewed *Claudette.* To be noticed by him at all is a big deal, and he wasn't too hard on you compared to what he wrote about Scott Nash."

"Caldwell! What an asshole! Okay, maybe Scott's not as great as he thinks he is, just because he was on *Oprah* six years ago, but Caldwell's rotten tomatoes review was pure revenge. Last year the old goat had a crush on Scott, whose interests don't lie at all in that direction, believe me." Tiffany looked cute when she was gossiping. "From what I hear, Scott wasn't even slightly diplomatic about refusing his advances. Big mistake! Caldwell's not somebody to get on the wrong side of. He'd probably do anything to get even."

Chapter Eighteen
No Suspects

"Surely that is an exaggeration," Mac said. "He would not, for example, kill?"

"What?" Tiffany Carmichael's blue eyes widened. "You mean like . . . what the hell?"

"Just a notion," Mac said. "It appears that someone is out to hurt the Erin Opera Company, but perhaps the opera is only collateral damage to some other purpose."

"What are you guys, like detectives or something?"

"Something," Lynda said. "Mac has cred along those lines, and I'm producing a podcast about this case for a news organization. Can I interview you?"

"Sure!"

For the next ten minutes Lynda expertly probed the soprano's thoughts and feelings about the tragedy at the Lyceum. For the record, Ms. Carmichael was shocked and horrified. She hadn't noticed anything suspicious backstage. And she hadn't learned about the murder until after the final curtain, when word had spread throughout the theater with the accustomed speed of all bad news.

"Did you know Aaron Schiff?"

"The dead guy? No. I mean, not by name. I may have seen him around the theater. I'm not sure."

Eventually the conversation circled back to Grayson Caldwell. "He'd give his mother a bad review if she crossed him," Ms. Carmichael insisted. "I hope I don't run into him around town."

"He is still in Erin?" Mac said. "That surprises me. Surely he must have other engagements."

"You would think, but I hear he's stalking Max Rohlfeld now."

This sounds like the plot of an opera.

Scott Nash and Max Rohlfeld had the two major male roles in *Claudette.*

"Well," my sister said, "we're happy to have you stay with us as long as you need to. But I'm sure Sebastian will clear up this matter in short order. Right, dear?" She gave Mac a Significant Look. She never calls him "dear."

"We can but try," he said.

Morrie Kindle of the Associated Press in Cincinnati, Joe "Call me Z" Ziebart of the online *Cincinnati Sentinel,* and the morning crew of Nadine Lattimore's Channel 11—not to mention Tall Rawls in the *Observer*—were all over the Schiff murder the next morning. Naturally, they focused on the possible connection with the high-profile Davenport homicide. Z, in particular, deftly suggested a link despite being unable to find anyone who could guess what it might be. Mac and Oscar were quoted in all the print accounts, which also included the mandatory expressions of dismay from Aaron Schiff's shocked neighbors. His family and fiancée apparently were too unraveled to talk to the media.

"I certainly hope that Mr. Schiff's affianced will overcome her grief enough to speak with us, Jefferson," Mac said. "Her knowledge could be crucial."

He had invaded my office that Monday morning, May 22, to discuss the case (after first reminding me that it was the birthday of Sir Arthur Conan Doyle). His appearance was a welcome break from dealing with veteran—make that elderly—*Observer* education reporter Maggie Barton. I love the old gal, but will she never retire? She was working on a story about the salaries of male and female faculty members at St. Benignus University, based on a story she'd seen about public universities in the *Chronicle of Higher Education*. What was the breakdown at SBU? I promised Maggie I would get back to her within twenty-four hours, even though we both knew that a private school wasn't obligated to share such data.

"You're a doll, Jeff," she'd said.

And then Mac had come in before I could ask the estimable Popcorn to get the necessary records from the Finance Office.

"I have an idea for a suspect," I told him after his opening salvo about Schiff's fiancée. I'd been waiting for this.

He raised an eyebrow. "Yes, Jefferson?"

"Sebastian McCabe."

Sebastian McCabe chuckled. "I thought we had ruled that out."

"Yes, but that was after only one murder. With the second, the evidence against you mounts. Now we strongly suspect that the killer's intent was to sandbag the Erin Opera Company. You yourself said the opera is an important tenant of Lafcadio Figg, or rather, of the non-profit which he created and still controls. Losing the opera as a tenant would hurt Figg's baby and therefore his pride. You and Figg can't stand each other approximately eighty-nine percent of the time. QED, you have a motive."

"Not even the credulous Lafcadio would believe that fairy tale, old boy."

"Then you won't mind that Lynda's talking to Figg this morning for her podcast?"

"Of course not. Why should I? However, I doubt the interview will be very enlightening. We have already established that Lafcadio has as much reason, or more, for wanting these murders solved as anyone else. Therefore, I am certain that if he had any relevant information he already would have shared it with Oscar or with me."

"What if he doesn't know what he knows, and even if he knows what he knows, he doesn't know that it's important?"

Mac looked thoughtful. "You may have a point, Jefferson." *Really? I don't even know what I just said.* "I will give that some further thought. For the nonce, however, let us consider the second victim, Aaron Schiff."

"From what I've read and heard," I said, "his situation sounds like just the opposite of Davenport in that he had no known enemies instead of a whole plethora of them." *I love the word plethora.* "That could support the theory that his murder was just misdirection from Davenport's death and the motive behind it. Or it could reinforce the premise that somebody wants to take down the Erin Opera Company."

"Or it could simply mean that Jordan Webster was the intended victim, as we initially assumed."

"I was just going to say that."

Mac called Oscar and caught him on the way out the door to talk to Schiff's grieving fiancée, Sally Henderson.

"Sure, join the party," he growled in response to Mac's request to horn in. "Hurry up. And bring a big handkerchief."

As he drove, Oscar informed us that the coroner believed the fatal wounds to Aaron Schiff were inflicted by the same knife or dagger that had killed Davenport.

"Dagger?" I repeated. "Maybe the killer was a pirate!"

"You mean one of the cast in *Claudette?*" Mac said. "I can assure you that their stage knives will barely cut butter."

"Oh."

It turned out that a metaphorical big handkerchief was unnecessary. Ms. Henderson was no weeping willow. She was processing her grief through anger.

"If I knew who killed Aaron, I'd cut the bastard's heart out," she declared through clinched teeth.

We spoke in a small conference room at the Shinkle Museum of Art, located on the better part of Front Street, a few blocks away from the Bijou. Sally Henderson worked there as the administrative assistant to Adam Mendenhall, the director. I remembered her from the day we had collected her boss's signature on the Save the Bijou ad. She was built like a ballet dancer, with a lean but powerful body. Her dark hair was pulled back into a pony tail, like Kendric Armstrong. I figured her to be in her late thirties, which would have made her about five years older than the man she had expected to marry in four months.

"It's even worse knowing that Aaron died for Jordan Webster," she added.

Mac raised an eyebrow. "Specifically, or generally?"

"What do you mean?"

"Is your anger deepened by the fact that your loved one apparently died in the place of someone else, or the fact that it was Mr. Webster whose place he took?"

"Oh, I see. Both, I guess. Jordan has a very high opinion of himself, which he sometimes tries to disguise with a false modesty that I find distasteful and irksome. Aaron and I didn't exactly socialize with him—Aaron was too far down the social ladder for that—but I met him a few times and that's the impression I always got."

"Starting an opera company in a town this size is no small feat," I pointed out. "Webster must have something on the ball."

"I didn't say he lacked ability. He has plenty of talent. If you don't believe me, just ask him."

Oscar cleared his throat. "Actually, we can't just rule out the possibility that your boyfriend was the killer's intended victim all along."

"What?" Her voice went up about an octave. "That's totally nuts. Everybody loved Aaron. He was the sweetest man in the world, the complete opposite of my waste-of-DNA ex. What makes you think anybody would want to kill him?"

"We don't necessarily think that. We're just exploring every possibility. And the fact is, somebody *did* kill him. Look, let's be frank, I'm sure you're aware that he had enough opioids in his apartment to stock a small pharmacy."

Mac raised an eyebrow. This was news to us. Oscar had been holding out!

"What's that supposed to mean?"

Oscar squirmed. "Well, a lot of killings are drug-related."

It was a good thing for Oscar that he was at the other end of a long table from Sally Henderson. The look she gave him would have frozen hellfire. "He had prescriptions to dull the pain from seven back operations over the past two years." Her voice rose. "He was riding his bike when he was hit by a drunk driver in a CRV. It was three o'clock on a Saturday afternoon. I'm sure you remember the case, *Chief.* One of your men arrested the driver on the spot. She was too plastered to flee the scene."

"Oh, yeah," Oscar mumbled. "Yeah, I do remember. I'd forgotten the name of the guy on the bike."

From the expression on Sally Henderson's face, that wasn't a good thing to admit. Mac tried a different tack:

"If Mr. Schiff was the intended target, not the victim of mistaken identity, the motive might have somehow related to the first murder. For example, is there any chance that your fiancé knew who killed Hunter Davenport?"

"I don't see how."

"Did he know Mr. Davenport?"

"Not so far as I know."

"He never mentioned him to you?"

"Only by way of saying he thought it was awful that Davenport blew into town and wanted to tear down the Bijou. He supported the Save-the-Bijou campaign and stuck yard signs outside his house and mine. It was kind of ironic that we just found out Davenport was sort of his boss."

"How's that?" Oscar asked before I could.

"Aaron had a side job working at Paddles & Wheels, that bike and canoe rental place. We read in the paper over the weekend that Davenport was a silent partner in the business. We didn't know that."

"Yes, he worked for me," Sheila Paxton said an hour or so later at her shop, looking vibrant in her *Paddles & Wheels* tank top. Oscar had gone back to his office for a scheduled meeting with Jordan Webster, who apparently was suffering high anxiety about being a potential murder target.

"Aaron was a teacher in real life and very responsible," the young entrepreneur went on. "He was always nice in the store, but I didn't really know him too well. I saw enough of the girlfriend to know that she was the jealous type, so I was careful to keep my distance. That's a good business practice anyway. Still, I was so sad to hear that he was killed. And how weird was that?"

"How weird was what?" I asked.

"I mean, two guys were murdered in Erin over the past few days and I knew both through business."

"Are you aware of any other link between the two men, besides you and the opera?" Mac asked.

My bet was that if there had been, Sally Henderson would have known.

Sheila Paxton mulled the question, then shook her head. "I can't imagine what it would be. I don't know whether they even knew each other. They didn't connect here so far as I know, unless Mr. Davenport ran into Aaron when he stopped by one day. But Mr. Davenport wasn't in the shop a lot."

"So, his death hasn't disrupted anything for you," I said. *In fact, you are better off because now you own the whole thing. Maybe Aaron Schiff figured that out, too!* That idea came to me out of nowhere, but I thought it had promise. Ms. Paxton's employee could have stumbled onto something and decided to squeeze her with it for a big wedding present. Never mind that she was attractive, smart, and no doubt kind to children and animals.

"Well, it's all been pretty jarring, of course," she said, "but it hasn't changed anything for me in the day-to-day operations. This is a pretty simple business. What I learned from Mr. Davenport was on the back end and marketing, and I think I've got that down now."

See above.

"In a way, I'll miss Aaron more. He's the one I have to replace."

"Mr. Schiff was quite an opera aficionado, as I understand," Mac commented. That seemed out of the blue until I realized what he was circling toward.

"He would have to be, I guess, to want to volunteer for it. But I didn't know that until the murder. It's not like he sang at work, or even talked about opera."

"I have enjoyed operas in New York, Paris, Milano, and Cincinnati, and I must say that *Claudette* was quite a creditable performance. Do you agree?"

She offered up a shrug and a winsome smile. "Don't ask me. I like the Beatles and church hymns. Opera doesn't interest me at all. I only went to the premiere because Aaron gave me a free ticket the day before. He said his fiancée had a last-minute conflict. It was all right, I guess."

"Where were you during the opera's final performance?" I asked.

She looked from one to the other of us, as if she had finally realized that we weren't asking questions out of idle curiosity. "Sunday afternoon? I was at choir practice at my church, Glad Tidings. Am I a suspect or something?"

Not "or something."

"I will be candid, Ms. Paxton," Mac said. "Apparently the same person killed Hunter Davenport, who had many enemies, and Aaron Schiff, who by all accounts had none. It seems likely that Jordan Webster was marked for the latter murder and escaped by happenstance, but that is by no means certain. Chief Hummel is seeking someone who had a reason to kill both Davenport and Webster, or Davenport and Schiff, or who wanted to sink the Erin Opera Company with bad publicity on top of lost financial sponsorship."

"You mean, like, put the opera out of business? That's nuts! Who would want to do a thing like that?"

"Who indeed? That is the great enigma."

Chapter Nineteen
Target for Murder

Over a late lunch, Lynda gave us the highlights of her podcast interview with Figg. She'd floated to him the idea that, since both murders potentially hurt the Lyceum—and therefore him—maybe that had been the point. Figg had shot down the notion.

"Essentially, he said he hasn't an enemy in the world."

Mac guffawed.

"He didn't know either murder victim," Lynda continued, "but he gave me some great background on the Lyceum which I think I can interweave with other materials as I set the scene of the murder. Oops, that reminds me." She looked at the time on her smartphone. "I meet Jordan Webster at the theater in fifteen minutes. Want to come along?"

"Certainly," Mac replied. "I spoke briefly with Oscar a short while ago, right after Mr. Webster's visit with him at the police station. That is one anxious young man. He demanded to know what Oscar is doing to protect him."

"And what is Oscar doing to protect him?" Lynda asked.

Mac shrugged his massive shoulders. "His capacity for that is limited, as Mr. Webster understands all too well. Colonel Gibbons and the other officers are keeping an eye on his residence as time allows. That cannot continue indefinitely, however. The need to unmask this particular murderer is more urgent than most."

"That isn't made any easier by the fact that the murderer may have worn a literal mask," I noted gloomily.

"Or maybe not," Lynda said.

"Do we not all wear masks at times?" Mac ruminated, veering off into philosophy. "Think of those lines in Eliot's 'Love Song of J. Alfred Prufrock': 'There will be time, there will be time/ To prepare a face to meet the faces that you meet.'"

"As Sherlock Holmes once said, 'Cut the poetry, Watson.'" That was Lynda, not me, though I appreciated the intervention. "This isn't the time for it."

And yet, Lynda herself turned somewhat poetic when she created a word portrait for her future podcast listeners a half-hour or so later at the murder scene.

"We meet Jordan Webster on the empty stage of the Lyceum Theater, just a few yards away from the murder scene," she intoned in NPR fashion into her recording device as Webster watched. "The sets have been dismantled and the stage is virtually bare except for a few costumes and props ready to be stored away for some future performance. Our voices echo slightly as we speak."

She turned off the device and thanked Webster for being patient. "I wanted to get that out of the way. Are you ready to talk on the record?"

"Sure. I've been working on the teardown today, but there's no real rush. The theater is dark until that benefit magic show in six or seven weeks."

Webster wore a black T-shirt and the state of his jeans indicated that he'd been up close and personal with taking apart the sets. When we had entered the theater, it struck me how small and vulnerable he looked on the empty stage. The weary gray eyes behind his round glasses looked like those of a man well past his age of twenty-nine.

"Good. Let's go, then." Lynda turned the digital recorder back on. "I understand that you met with Chief

Hummel today at your request. Can you say what that was about?"

"Somebody wants to kill me. I want to be sure that whoever it is gets caught before he succeeds. I heard that the Erin police are asking questions about Aaron's murder as if he was the intended victim all along. I went to tell the Chief that's a complete waste of time. I was the real target, not Aaron."

He held up the front page of Friday's *Observer*. Lynda described his action for her podcast listeners.

"Here I am on the front page of the paper dressed in the costume Aaron wore when he was killed," Webster continued. "That's me under the Baron Samedi top hat. The caption under the photo says so. What that means is that anybody who saw this would have thought that was me backstage, preparing to go on in the second act."

"Why would somebody want to kill you?"

Webster didn't hesitate.

"A week ago, I would have had no idea. But coming after the murder of our presenting sponsor, it's clear that the killer is trying to sabotage the Erin Opera Company. The first attempt, aimed at cutting off our funding, failed because Nadine Lattimore generously stepped up. That made it necessary for the killer to take the more direct approach of going after me. Without me, there is no Erin Opera."

Webster was singing a familiar tune here, but for a new audience—Lynda's podcast.

Mac—standing right next to me—pinged me with a text: *Apparently JW concurs with Sherlock Holmes: "I cannot agree with those who rank modesty among the virtues."* Look who was texting!

The interview went on, oblivious to this byplay:

"That begs the next question," Lynda said. "Who would want to shut down the opera company, and why?"

Storm clouds gathered over Webster's brow as he pondered that. "I'm not so sure I should speculate on the record. I could be wrong."

"What about Grayson Caldwell?" Lynda pressed. "He seemed rather harsh in his review."

Mac texted again: *Thin as tomato soup.*

"He wasn't grading on the curve, that's for sure," Webster said, "but I was just grateful that he gave us the attention. *Claudette*'s cast members might not be on board with that, I thought, what with the scathing review and the personal history that Caldwell had with Scott Nash, according to Tiffany Carmichael.

Lynda turned off the digital recorder. "Okay, I'll make you a deal. When I turn this back on, go ahead and speculate. Speculate your head off. The podcast won't come out until somebody has been tried and convicted for these murders. If your guess is wrong, I won't use it. Deal?"

He only thought for a few seconds. "I suppose that's fair enough."

Lynda turned the recorder back on and gave it another go:

"Who do you think wants to destroy the Erin Opera Company?"

"I don't have a name in mind, but I've thought that maybe it was my counterpart at some other small opera company in the region. Maybe I've been too successful at attracting top talent."

Skepticism was written all over my wife's lovely face. "Wouldn't murder be a pretty drastic response to healthy competition?"

"Sure. But you have to remember that we're dealing with the world of opera, which Samuel Johnson defined as 'an exotick and irrational entertainment.' In my experience, I could be having a calm discussion with a prima donna and all of a sudden we're in the last act of *Madame Butterfly*, lots of emotion."

Great stuff, Lynda must have been thinking, judging by her satisfied expression.

"You are obviously very concerned for your life," she told Webster.

"Yes, I am."

"I understand that the Erin police are watching your home."

"They're doing the best they can, I'm guess, but it's a small force."

"What are you doing to protect yourself?"

"I'm being very, very careful."

With a sly look, Webster stuck his hand into his right jeans pocket and slid out a gun that fit neatly into his hand. Mac told me later it was something called a Beretta Pico. He slid it back without a word.

Lynda turned off the recorder and thanked him. This is the point at which some reporters ask the gotcha questions, when the subject's defenses are down. But Lynda doesn't play that game. She never did. I know that because in the early days of our acquaintanceship she was a reporter at the *Observer* and I was a source. Eventually I realized that a lot of our conversations had nothing to do with business.

Anyway, her interview was well and truly over when she turned off the recorder. But Mac's wasn't. "Do you know Dr. David Hawthorne?" he asked Webster.

"Why, yes. He's a significant supporter. Nowhere near the Hunter Davenport level, but significant. He's the first one listed in the program under 'Other Supporters'— Anonymous. Why do you ask?"

"I was merely verifying what he told us. That is a habit of mine—confirming apparently insignificant statements."

Mac stooped toward a cluster of overflowing boxes on the stage floor, no easy task for him. Props stuck out of some boxes; costumes spilled over the tops of others.

"Please don't—" Webster began, but he stopped cold when Mac picked up a white skull mask. It was part of the Baron Samedi costume that Aaron Schiff had worn at the time of his death, apparently returned to its owner by the coroner's office. We'd just seen it in that *Observer* photograph.

"Would it be too fanciful to call this a death mask?" Mac mused.

"Yes," Lynda and I responded in chorus.

Chapter Twenty
Confessions of a Critic

"No, absolutely not," Grayson Caldwell declared. "I do not grant interviews."

Lynda made a production out of putting away her digital recorder. "I'm sorry you feel that way. I've been a fan of your reviews for years."

Caldwell, sitting with us over coffee in the restaurant of the elegant Winfield Hotel in late afternoon, seemed to take that as no more than his due. He didn't acknowledge the compliment.

"Surely it has not been that many years, young lady."

Apparently, Caldwell would hit on anybody, as long as he or she was good-looking. He himself, I must admit, was a reasonably attractive specimen of the over-sixty set, except that his auburn toupee was slightly askew and the elegant tailoring of his Armani suit failed to conceal the extra thirty pounds or so around his middle.

"I'm half-Italian," Lynda informed him. "My *nonna* started taking me to the opera when I was very small."

Also, an opera—or a soap opera—could have been written about Lynda's mother. I made a mental note to talk to Luther Kressel about that.

"When I agreed to meet you, I didn't realize that you would be bringing two gentlemen along," Caldwell complained. *Cramping your style, are we?*

Lynda had called him because this was her show. She wanted to meet the opera maven.

"Jeff is my husband and Mac is our brother-in-law," she explained.

"Oh." Caldwell managed to invest the single syllable with a mixture of disdain and disappointment. Upon first sitting down with Caldwell, Lynda had only dished out our names. She'd given hers as Lynda Teal because she was on the clock for the podcast.

"They aren't just along for the ride. The podcast I'm working on is about the murders of Hunter Davenport and Aaron Schiff, which Mac is going to solve." She launched into a recital of Mac's crime-solving chops, highlighting the internationally reported murders of Peter Gerard in Erin and Arthur James Phillimore in London. Mac tried to look modest while Caldwell struggled to seem unimpressed. Neither succeeded.

"I suppose you were hoping my name would not be unfamiliar to your audience," Caldwell said. "I can think of no other reason that you would wish to interview me."

Mac was happy to enlighten him. "I think you have more to offer our inquiries than that, Mr. Caldwell. The connection between the two murders is the opera—specifically, the Erin Opera Company. One promising theory is that someone wants to sabotage that noble effort."

Caldwell's chuckle seemed a bit forced to me. "I should think that it would perish of self-inflicted wounds." I had the feeling that he was proud of his on-the-spot wordsmithing.

"You were pretty harsh in your review," Lynda pointed out.

"If you are truly a follower of my oeuvre, Ms. Teal, you know that I never pull punches. The libretto and the score were better than I expected, but everything else was subpar even for this little burg."

Since "everything else" included Kate's costumes and set design, I give Mac and me credit for not coming across the table at the pompous poseur.

"Henry Knox Wilcox found the entire production 'of major company quality'," Lynda quoted.

"Who?"

"Never mind."

"Why did you come to 'this little burg' to begin with?" I asked, testing to see whether he would allude to his relationship with Scott Nash. And, by golly, he did! Sort of.

He spread his hands in a gesture of magnanimity. "I was familiar with some of the cast members and knew that they were not untalented. All the more reason for my disappointment that the artistic director did not bring out the best in them." *So, it's Jordan Webster's fault!* But maybe Caldwell was right about that. How would I know?

"In particular," Mac said casually, "we understand that you had once, let us say, attempted an affectional relationship with Scott Nash, who played the villainous de Lubac."

Caldwell didn't even blink. He gets points for that in my book. "The opera gossip mill never stops churning, does it? Well, I see no reason to deny that I had hoped that Scott would be more receptive to my interest than he was some months ago."

"But Nash wasn't having any," Lynda said.

Caldwell shrugged, trying to telegraph indifference. "Though crudely put, that is accurate, Ms. Teal. These things happen. And they have happened to me often enough that they long ago ceased to cloud my professional judgement. You see, I anticipate the rest of the gossip—the implication that my negative review was spite-driven. Nonsense. I assure you that I gave the performance of *Claudette* that I witnessed exactly the criticism that it deserved. Scott richly merited my harsh words."

Lynda looked slightly pained. "I have to admit that he was a bit of a disappointment. Which is a shame because his character was a great operatic villain."

"As I recall, Mr. Caldwell, you wrote that Scott Nash 'sang like a crow with a bad hangover,'" Mac put in.

"Did you like that line?"

"Since you asked, I must say in truth that it sounds like the tortured phrasing of a man intoxicated by his own cleverness." *Good one, Mac!* "That happens to the best writers occasionally, even my friend Jefferson." *Hey, wait!* "However, Lynda did not seek an interview to discuss your literary style. An imaginative mind—such as mine—could construct a scenario in which your animus toward Mr. Nash extended to the Erin Opera Company for retaining his services."

Caldwell turned from smug to huffy. "There was no animus."

"Where were you yesterday during the final performance of *Claudette?*"

"After failing to reach a rapprochement with Scott, and then being rebuffed by another member of the cast, I spent the whole afternoon nursing my wounded vanity at a watering hole with the banal name of The Speakeasy."

"Alone?"

"It started out that way, but I made the acquaintance of a very pleasant waitress of middle years." The self-satisfaction on Caldwell's face pained me. "She can verify my whereabouts for the rest of the evening—until this morning, in fact."

"I hardly think that will be necessary."

"Do you have any idea who would want to take down the Erin Opera Company?" I asked, just because somebody had to.

"An opera lover, perhaps."

Chapter Twenty-One
Media Alert

"Blessed are they who expect little, for they shall not be disappointed," I consoled Lynda the next day during the three-ring circus that is breakfast at Chez Cody.

"But I *am* disappointed, darling. The podcast is going nowhere fast."

"Well, you couldn't have expected much out of Caldwell. It was never very likely that he even knew who Hunter Davenport was, much less that he had any hand in killing him to get revenge on Scott Nash."

"No, but I'd hoped he would add a little glamour to the story. But he was such a jerk, it's just as well that he wouldn't let me record. Everything he had to say was so . . . unsavory."

"He should go into politics," I said. That morning's *Observer* carried a photo of Bruce Gordon, as promised, amending his campaign paperwork to name Davenport as the man behind the LLC's shoveling money into his mayoral campaign. His opponents were not placated, offering up boilerplate quotes about buying the election. Lani Alvarez promised that she would have more to say soon about recent events. Inside the paper, Bijou supporters and non-incumbent City Council candidates were still yapping about the illegal texting by Council's Gang of Five.

"How does all this political theater relate to the murders, if at all, Jefferson?" Mac demanded later in his office, the newspaper spread out in front of him.

"Don't ask me. I just work here."

And believe me, trying to explain to the *Observer*'s superannuated Maggie Barton why female professors at SBU earn 85 percent of what male professors earn was real work. I had a call in to the Provost, thinking it might be a good idea to have her offer Maggie a few quotes as well.

"It seems quite a coincidence that a man so heavily involved in politics as Hunter Davenport should be murdered just as his contributions—and the quid pro quo that he likely expected from their beneficiary—became controversial," Mac rumbled on. "Coincidences are always suspect. In real life they do happen, of course, although they are *verboten* in fiction. However, if Mr. Davenport's demise was politically motivated, what of Aaron Schiff's?" Mac shook his leonine head. "So far as we know after all our questioning, the Erin Opera Company and Paddles & Wheels are the only connections between the two victims."

"Sheila Paxton!" I exclaimed. "I'd almost forgotten about her. Next to Nadine Lattimore, she's the biggest beneficiary of Davenport's murder. There's no reason she couldn't have been Pinkerton in that surveillance video, based on her body type. And if she killed her partner, their employee could have been in a good position to find out about it and blackmail her."

"I really must congratulate you, Jefferson." Mac beamed as though his pet Labrador had performed a particularly cute trick. "Your logic is faultless. In fact, I had thought along those lines myself. I asked Oscar to be particularly diligent about checking Ms. Paxton's assertion that she was at choir practice during the time of the second murder. At least two dozen fellow congregants will swear that she was, plus an assistant pastor."

"Oh." Then I had a thought: "What about a boyfriend?"

"She has none. Colonel Gibbons investigated that as well. All her friends agree that the choir has been her entire social life since she started her business. She even dropped out of active participation in the bicycle club that she helped found."

"You could have told me that earlier," I muttered.

"I should have. I apologize."

"Accepted. What are you going to do next?"

Mac drummed his fingers on the desk. "If I were Nero Wolfe, I would create a charade designed to unmask the killer."

"Well, you aren't Nero Wolfe. Or Sherlock Holmes, for that matter. But you *are* Sebastian McCabe."

"There is that, old boy."

"Then do your thing!"

Feeling I had provided a useful service with this badgering, and having nothing else to offer, I made that my exit line. I went back to my office to see what wonders Popcorn had performed in my absence. Within a few moments, the Provost was on the line returning my call. I brought her up to speed on Maggie's salary story.

"The reason female teachers at BSU are paid less, on average, than their male counterparts is that fewer of them are full professors with tenure," I informed her. "I'll e-mail you the data. The numbers don't lie, but they tell more than one story."

"I don't like either story," Saylor-Mackie said.

But she agreed to call the old trouper back since she would have more credibility than me on gender-based pay disparity.

"It could be worse," I told the Provost. "As Popcorn pointed out, at least she's not comparing coaches' salaries to professors'."

"Or to mine," Lesley Saylor-Mackie said dryly. "You know, Jeff, this isn't just a PR problem."

"It hardly ever is."

"What do you mean?"

The Thomas Jefferson Cody College of Communications is now in session. How many times had I tried to explain this to Ralph without success?

"Whenever a company or institution gets into trouble, you will hear the phrase 'bad PR.' And then, sooner or later, people up the food chain from whoever handles communications will start babbling about the need to 'put a positive spin on this.' What they don't get is that some pigs resist lipstick."

"Meaning?"

"More often than not, the hitch isn't the way the facts are presented, but the facts themselves. Somebody, or several somebodies, screwed up. And people of ordinary intelligence are insulted by messaging that tries to paper over the screw-up—the kind of baloney you get from politicians on the Sunday morning talk shows. In this case, trying to deny what the numbers show would add insult to injury. The best we can do is provide Maggie with additional information that puts an unfortunate situation into context."

I could almost hear Saylor-Mackie nodding thoughtfully over the phone. "What you say makes perfect sense, Jeff. But when it comes to this issue of faculty salaries, there is one other thing I now have the power to do now that I'm Provost."

"What's that?"

"Change the facts going forward so we don't have the same kind of salary disparity—and tenure disparity— five years from now. I'll start working on a plan to do that. I only wish Warren Burch were as easy to deal with."

Burch always reminded me of Lex Luthor or Daddy Warbucks. His head was balder than a billiard ball, not shaved but naturally hairless. He'd been a member of the SBU faculty for forty-three years, most recently as dean of the Gulliver Mackie School of Business and Economics. The faculty of the school had adopted a resolution of "no confidence" in him because of his dictatorial way of running things. Sometimes that happens when people have been around so long they confuse themselves with the institution.

Saylor-Mackie had been loath to remove him from the deanship despite his leadership problems because she and he had been at odds ever since she'd been appointed Provost. He'd even publicly suggested, bizarrely, that she'd only received the position because her husband had donated so much money to the business school that the directors had named it after him. Saylor-Mackie therefore feared that any action she took against Burch would seem vindictive. But the faculty vote of no confidence changed that.

"He's got to go," she told me. "In addition to the way he treats faculty, I just learned that three female work-study students over the years have accused him of such actions as leering, making them bend over to pick things up, and asking for dance lessons. Burch denies it, and we can't prove it, but I believe it. Those three women are no longer at St. Benignus. We let them down. I'm pissed."

Lesley Saylor-Mackie doesn't talk like that. I picked my jaw back up off the floor to ask, "Did Burch touch any of them or force them to do anything sexual?"

"No."

"Well, he's still a skank. I'll leave the legal advice on dealing with him to Kelly Richards, since she's our counsel. But from a public image point of view—and I'm sorry to say this—you'd be wise to negotiate a settlement that gives Burch a load of cash, a teaching sinecure with no work-study students, and lavish praise for a job well done."

"I bristle at the thought, Jeff."

"Who wouldn't? But if you don't go down that road, you'll eventually have to settle a highly publicized lawsuit at an even higher cost. And you may wind up paying the jerk's attorney fees."

We were just winding up the call when my beloved spouse pinged me: *Alvarez holding news conference outside Lyceum about murders. Join the fun?*

She had to ask?

Lynda was already waiting, along with Johanna Rawls and Sam Sams. The latter was a student intern at SBU radio station WIJC, working with station veteran Tony Lampwicke. Maybe he thought it would be nice to get out of the newsroom. No other media were in attendance, nor was mayoral candidate Lani Alvarez.

"Any guess what this is about?" Tall Rawls asked the world at large.

"I don't know," Lynda said, "but I hope she gives us some good sound bites for the podcast."

"It won't be dull," I predicted.

After about five minutes, the star of the show arrived. Her dyed-yellow and straightened hair was pulled behind her ears. She wore stone-washed jeans, two-hundred-dollar Nikes, and a fierce look, but no bra. She marched up the three front steps of the Lyceum and struck a pose. Johanna took her photo with a smartphone.

"Thank you all for coming, even those of you who are not media." Alvarez spoke as though she were addressing a crowd. "I stand here today as a candidate for mayor and an innocent woman. I categorically deny any involvement in the murders of Hunter Davenport and Aaron Schiff. I didn't even know them personally."

Mac raised an eyebrow.

Lynda held out her digital recorder. "Has somebody accused you?"

"There are rumors."

There always are.

"What possible reason would you have for killing the victims?" Johanna asked.

Alvarez stiffened her back and raised her voice to reach the small audience of gawkers that was gathering to watch the show. "I abhor violence, but these two beneficiaries of white privilege were far from innocent. Hunter Davenport was a capitalist fool who contributed thousands of ill-gotten dollars to one of my opponents, Bruce Gordon, because he knows that when I am mayor, our administration will put people over profits. Also, he helped to fund the culturally insensitive opera performed here." She gestured at the theater behind her with an arm. "Aaron Schiff was complicit in that injustice as well, and the apparent intended victim Jordan Webster most of all."

"Speak of the devil," I whispered to Mac. Not that Webster was a devil, but just at that moment he and Nadine Lattimore emerged from the front door of the Lyceum.

"What's going on here?" Webster demanded.

"I'm holding a news conference to defend myself from scurrilous charges," Alvarez said.

"Scurrilous?" Nadine repeated. "That's rich, coming from you. I heard what you just said about my husband."

The broadcaster had probably attended hundreds of news conferences in her career before moving up to the anchor desk, but this was likely the only one she'd stumbled onto by accident. No doubt it was also the only one that hit so close to home.

Sam Sams, a geeky-looking guy with a pencil figure and horn-rimmed glasses, moved in closer with his microphone so he didn't miss anything.

"Did I say something that wasn't true?" Alvarez asked, all innocence. "Wasn't he a capitalist? Didn't he contribute to Bruce Gordon's mayoral campaign, while hiding behind the names of shell companies?"

Nadine got up close and personal with the candidate, who was about a foot shorter. "My husband also made many generous contributions to this community during the short time he was a part of it, often anonymously." Her voice quivered. "You have no idea what you're talking about." She didn't actually add "you bitch," but that was the tone of it.

"Hunter was also a generous supporter of opera in this community, which you did your feeble best to cripple." Webster tried to stare down Alvarez, a noble cause but a lost one; the woman was impenetrable. "You're despicable. What gives you the right to stand on these steps and spout that garbage?"

"The Constitution of the United States. I am exercising my right to free speech."

How long is Mac going to stay silent here?

"Actually, Ms. Alvarez, the Constitution is not a factor in this travesty," Mac said mildly. "The First Amendment prohibits *the government* from abridging one's freedom of speech, to which case law has established such exceptions as sedition, obscenity, and libel. By no means, however, does that cherished freedom mean that an American citizen has the right to speak anywhere at any time. You happen to be on private property, owned by the Lyceum Theater Corp. Should the president of that non-profit object to your presence here, you will have to leave or be guilty of trespassing."

It wouldn't be the first time.

Alvarez made a show of looking around. "Is that person here?"

"I can call him." Webster whipped out his cell phone.

"You'll regret that," Alvarez muttered.

"If you're trying to establish your innocence in the murders, this is a damned funny way to do it," came a familiar-sounding voice out of the crowd. "You just made it clear you hated the victims." I'd had the same thought myself. I turned around. Reginald Fortesque III, scrappy as ever and dressed in a natty blue blazer, stood a few feet behind me.

Alvarez arranged her face into an expression of surprise as phony as the color of her hair. "I told you I am a non-violent person. Besides, I was picketing on this very sidewalk at the times of both murders. You can ask anybody who was there."

Chapter Twenty-Two
A Widow's Lonely Walk

After that, things broke up quickly. Lani Alvarez had accomplished her mission.

"You hear the term 'publicity stunt' all the time, but that may be the first time I've ever actually seen one," Lynda said.

I concurred. "She called a news conference to dispute allegations that don't exist—just so she could get some coverage out of it to the benefit, she thinks, of her mayoral campaign."

"Ingenious!" Mac boomed.

"It sure is. Not that I would ever do anything like that for the university. It's not honest. Plus, playing such games always comes back to bite you in the rear."

Lynda wasn't around to hear that because she had left our side to dog Nadine and Webster, who were chatting their way down the street. With my longer legs, I caught up to them about the same time that Lynda did. At least, I was close enough to hear her hail them.

"Ms. Lattimore, I wonder if I could talk to you for a few minutes?"

She turned around, looking at my wife with an expression on her weary face that was by no means unfriendly. "You're Lynda Teal, aren't you?"

"That's right."

"I saw you Sunday afternoon, here at the theater, but we didn't have a chance to talk. I hope you and station management can work out that media partnership you're talking about. I grew up reading the *Observer*, so I would love to have Channel Eleven connected to it."

"I would like that as well. It would be an honor to be associated with your news operation." She paused, then dove in: "I'm so sorry about your husband. I can't even imagine what you're going through, and Ms. Alvarez's farce could only make it worse. But I wonder if you'd be ready to talk to me for a podcast we're doing about the murder. It's not for immediate distribution. It won't be aired until after the killer is caught, tried, and sentenced."

"I don't think—" began Jordan Webster, standing at Nadine's side.

She shot him a glance, not approving, and answered for herself: "Yes, I'll do that. Lord knows I've asked plenty of other grieving loved ones to do something similar for the camera. I hate it that so often news people give a 'no comment' when the story is about them. Besides, this might be cathartic for me."

Lynda beamed. "Great! Would you mind doing it at the *Observer* offices? There's a small room with good acoustics. It's best to record there, except when the ambient sounds of a location are important to telling the story."

Just a few weeks into this podcast project, Lynda was already talking like a pro at it.

Nadine agreed and expressed no objection to the firm of McCabe & Co., the "Co." being me, tagging along. If Jordan Webster expected to be invited to join the party, he must have been disappointed. The last we saw of him that afternoon he was getting into his silver-gray Hyundai.

Once we had settled in at the *Observer* with coffee and conversation, Lynda turned on the recorder and got down to business. She began with taking Nadine back to her feelings on the night of her husband's murder.

"I was in denial at first." The widow spoke slowly. "This is the kind of thing that happens to other people, certainly not to me. I've always been in control of my life and everything's gone just the way I wanted—all the big stuff, anyway. And frankly, I like being in control. I suppose that's why I married so late. And Hunter died so suddenly, so cruelly, it felt awful to not be in control of my life anymore." She gripped her coffee cup ("*The Erin Observer & News Ledger*—Your Source for Local News") as if it were a life preserver. "It was all so surreal, the idea that this was happening to me. When it finally sunk in, there was this immense sense of loss, like I was in a black ocean. I felt so alone, and lonely. Then I was consumed by anger at whoever did this, and at God for letting it happen."

When she stopped talking, the little room was so utterly silent that I could almost hear Nadine swallowing her coffee. I wondered whether she tasted it. Her green eyes glistened.

After what seemed like a long time, but was probably twenty seconds or so, Lynda said, "Just for the record, who do you think killed your husband?"

Nadine sighed. "I wake up at night in an empty bed wondering about that. I gave Chief Hummel some names of people Hunter had crossed swords with, but only because he pressed me. I don't really want to speculate. It's bad enough that people are talking about me—I know they are. The mindless nastiness of it is devastating. So, no, I don't want to point any fingers in Hunter's death."

"And then came the murder of Aaron Schiff," Lynda said in a funereal tone. "Do you know of any connection between him and your husband?"

"But he wasn't the intended victim!"

"Probably not, but we don't know for sure."

"That poor man and Jordan both had the same connection to Hunter—the Erin Opera Company. Of course, Hunter knew Jordan fairly well, while I have no reason to think he knew Aaron Schiff at all. I'd certainly never heard the name until Sunday."

There was another connection, Paddles & Wheels, but I presumed the point of Lynda's question was to find out if Nadine knew that, or if there was another link between the two men as well.

"The death of a spouse is always a life-changing event in the best of circumstances," Lynda said. "What are you going to do next?"

"I've taken an open-ended leave of absence from Channel Eleven while I work that out. I offered to sell my share in the Paddles & Wheels rental business to Sheila Paxton, the majority owner, but she asked me to stay involved and help her run the business. That has its attraction to me as a productive change of pace. I used to ride bikes with Hunter. He thought the business could really take off if the city extended the bike trail along the Ohio. He was advocating for the acquisition of seven miles of unused rail track from the E&O Railway for the purpose. You may recall that's one of the issues City Council members were discussing in violation of the sunshine law."

I was surprised that Nadine brought up that sunshine law can of worms, but she moved on quickly:

"What I'm not going to do is keep Davenport Development. I'm getting not-so-subtle pressure from construction companies and city boosters to push ahead with the Bijou project, but I've already made it clear that's not going to happen."

Good thing you didn't say "over my dead body."

Mac cleared his throat and shot my spouse a meaningful look. She nodded slightly, the green light to take over the interview. After all, the theme of the podcast was supposed to be a Sebastian McCabe mystery.

"The demise of the project upon your husband's death was, if not inevitable, at least possible," Mac observed, just in case she had missed the obvious. "While chronological sequence alone can never prove cause and effect, it can be strongly indicative. The hypothesis that someone killed your husband to prevent the demolition of the Bijou Theatre is, regrettably, a natural one."

"Sure," Nadine said. "But I'm sure you didn't do it, even though you benefited from it, as I pointed out in Chief Hummel's office on Friday. And I'm equally sure that if one of your save-the-Bijou crowd killed Hunter, you would grant him no quarter."

With all that butter she was spreading, I figured she was either (a) trying to get away with murder or (b) hoping to land an exclusive TV interview with Mac when she came back from her leave of absence. I had no idea which. Mac, taking her statement as no more than a convenient truth, rolled on:

"The waters have been muddied, however, by the murder of Aaron Schiff, apparently by the same hand. Mr. Schiff's life intersected with your husband's more than just through the opera. Although he was a teacher, he also had a part-time job working at Paddles & Wheels."

"He did? I didn't know that!"

"It was reported in the *Observer*," I pointed out.

Nadine shook her head. "I've been avoiding news coverage on the murders, whether in print or on the air. It's just too raw for me."

Chapter Twenty-Three
A Masque of Masks

"Well, at least she gave us a new angle," Lynda said after Nadine had left.

"And that would be . . . ?" Mac prompted.

"The proposal to extend the riverfront bike trail! Davenport was pushing for that and City Council members were talking about it behind metaphorical closed doors. Maybe that's why somebody blew the whistle to Manny Templeton about the texting —to put the kibosh on the bike trail, not the Bijou plan. And maybe that somebody got impatient with the results of Templeton's activities and decided to solve the problem with a knife, used repeatedly."

"Like who, for instance?" I said. "Who would be violently opposed to adding a few miles to the bike path?" It sounded like a great idea to me.

"Somebody's whose business or lifestyle would be seriously cramped by a bunch of bikers maybe? How should I know? Mac's the genius here!"

He didn't deny it.

"The identity of Mr. Templeton's source of information, presumably someone close to one of the participants in those extra-legal virtual discussions, continues to interest me," he ruminated. "The unknown tipster was certainly no friend of Hunter Davenport."

"A lot of people weren't," I noted helpfully.

Mac and I said little more to each other as we rode in his Chevy back to campus, each absorbed in his own thoughts. While Mac presumably had murder on his mind, I was trying to calculate whether the arrival of two additional dependent children would mean that Lynda and I should take the standard deduction instead of itemizing on our federal tax return. Before I could reach a best guess on that, we were at the SBU parking lot.

"Luther Kressel," I exclaimed.

"What about him, old boy?"

"He's right over there." Luther was conspicuous for his nearly hairless dome and white goatee, possibly swiped off a billy goat, and for the ever-present Bluetooth in his ear. "Think about this, Mac: Luther's first opera is going to be best known for being marred by murder, and the opera company has lost its primary patron. That means he's another victim of the killer."

"Only in the most expansive . . ."

But I was already out of the car and hailing Luther, whom I hadn't seen since opening night. I didn't think Mac had, either.

Our campus polymath turned around and put a smile on his face. "Oh, hi, Jeff. Hey, I wanted publicity for *Claudette*, but not like this. I'm just gutted about that young man's murder."

If your title is "director of communications," which everybody shortens to "PR guy," you tend to hear a lot of lame jokes about publicity.

"As a matter of fact," I said, "I don't think the murders did you any good at all. Did you ever think about that?"

His expressive face showed puzzlement. "What do you mean?"

"Jefferson has been seized with the notion that two murders were committed to thwart your budding career in opera," Mac said with keen insight into my thought process. But he sounded skeptical.

Luther gaped.

Okay, if you put it that way, it does sound a little far-fetched.

"I wouldn't put it that way," I said.

"How would you put it?" Mac asked.

Luther spared me from having to answer by tossing in his own question. "Who the hell would do that?"

Do I have to draw you a map? "How about Lani Alvarez? She didn't picket *Claudette* because she wanted to boost ticket sales."

"No, she just did that because she hates me."

Mac raised an eyebrow. "Not for the stated reason that she found your work politically incorrect?"

"Well, maybe she believed the crap she was dishing out on the picket line, but she's also one to hold a grudge. And I'm sure she's still honked that I gave her a failing grade in Economics 101 a couple of years back when she was one of my most intransigent students."

"There you are!" I said.

"Killing two people to avenge a lamentable grade seems a bit excessive, does it not?" Mac said dubiously. "Especially when the victims were not the offenders."

"Maybe she wanted Luther to suffer by seeing his opera go down in flames and lose his chance to have others produced."

"I'm not planning any more operas, anyway," Luther said. "I told Alvarez that when I saw her picketing on opening night. So, I have no 'budding opera career' for her to ruin."

"Oh. Well, why not?"

"Because I'm working on a symphony for the Southwest Ohio Philharmonic. I've never written a symphony."

This wasn't going well for my half-formed, or maybe half-baked, theory.

"Lynda will be disappointed," I said. "She loved *Claudette*."

"As did I," Mac announced.

"Well, thank you both. All in a day's work, while not teaching economics and history. I think it turned out okay, but it wasn't easy. At first, I thought of making it a tale of hubris and a tragic flaw, like Greek drama or *Macb*—"

"The Scottish play," I inserted.

"Right. Well, you know, in classical drama a tragic flaw is the character weakness in an otherwise great figure which destroys him in the end, sort of hoist with his own petard—ego, ambition, or whatever. But I decided to scrap that trope and go with a tale of love and lust where the true villain appears to be respectable and the heroine's love interest is a rogue with a heart of gold. So, appearances are deceiving in *Claudette*, which is why both acts end at Mardi Gras with everybody in costume. I wanted to call the opera *Death Masque*, spelled m-a-s-q-u-e, with a nod toward Poe's 'Masque of the Red Death.'"

"Old-fashioned spelling?" I said.

"No, that's not the idea. A masque was a dramatic art form in Sixteenth and Seventeenth Century England in which masked players acted and danced."

How did I not know this? I bet Mac did.

"*Claudette* was a sort of masque in operatic form," he commented.

"Exactly. But Jordan wouldn't let me call it one. He said the title *Death Masque* didn't match his artistic vision for the opera. And who am I to argue, being merely the librettist and composer? Jordan said it needed a title reminiscent of similar operas with strong women, like *Aida*, *Carmen*, *Tosca*, *Elektra*."

"He would have been thinking of Strauss's *Elektra*, which is much different from the original Greek drama in which everyone on stage would have worn masks."

"I'm more of a Verdi and Puccini fan," Luther informed us. "I kind of stole the suicide by knife in the end from Puccini's *Madame Butterfly*. Butterfly does herself in with a hara-kiri knife because that caddish American naval officer—"

"Yes," Mac assured him, "we remember."

"Stabbing is popular in opera, you know."

"If you say so," I said, "but we're a tad more interested in some local knifework, Luther."

"Well, the murders have nothing to do with me. Even Kendric wouldn't go so far as to suggest that."

"Kendric Armstrong?" Mac said. "You have some conflict?"

"I don't want to make a mountain out of it, but his nose was bent a little out of shape because he's the drama guy at SBU and I'm the one who had an opera produced. He's dropped a few comments my way here and there, low-level stuff to remind me that I'm an amateur. Which I am. The word 'amateur' comes from the Latin, *amare*, so an amateur is one who loves what he does. No shame in that."

"Kendric gains from Davenport's death," I mused before Mac—the amateur sleuth—could expound on this lesson in etymology. "The saving of the Bijou means that it could become the new theater for SBU, just as Kendric and the Provost have talked about. Plus, Kendric donated money to Lani Alvarez's mayoral campaign, which put him and Davenport into different political camps."

Mac pondered. "And what about Aaron Schiff?"

"Maybe he was The Man Who Knew Too Much, like the second murder victim in approximately ninety-eight percent of all mystery novels."

You may wonder why the communications director of St. Benignus University was building a case against one of our own faculty members, which would be the worst publicity ever. Right now, I'm wondering the same thing. But that didn't occur to me in the flush of my new idea.

"Perhaps this is a notion that should not be prematurely abandoned," Mac conceded.

"You guys are kidding, right?" Luther said.

"Of course we are," I lied.

Kendric Armstrong's office is in Herbert Hall, a few floors away from Mac's. We found him in residence there, grading papers. Don't ask me why acting students need to write papers.

He looked up with a smile. "Hail fellows, well met."

"You're sounding pretty chipper," I said.

"I should be. The Provost gave me the go-head today to put together a specific plan to acquire the Bijou for my department. There are some big fat grants, public and private, just ready for the plucking for that kind of thing."

"You are moving with great dispatch," Mac noted.

"Damn right. If we act fast enough and loud enough, any potential competition may drop out before they're even in."

"Couldn't you at least wait until the body is cold?" I had my PR hat on. "The optics of jumping on this before murders are solved are terrible."

"Maybe so, but we have to jump before somebody beats us to it."

"You should be pleased that Hunter Davenport is no longer around to block your plans, ghoulish though that may be," Mac said mildly.

"Hmmm. I suppose that's so. Never thought of it that way. I guess it's a good thing I have an alibi for the time of his murder."

"You do?"

"Sure. I was on stage in *Claudette*. In fact, I was in every performance as one of the pirates. Arrr!"

I mentally thwacked myself in the head. "I saw you on opening night. You were easy to recognize—no mask or anything like that."

Kendric rubbed his facial hair. "I've always thought of my mustache as piratical."

"I saw but did not observe," Mac said.

Okay, so Kendric had a solid alibi for the first murder, the one where he benefited. He wouldn't have intended to kill Jordan Webster just because Webster had chosen to produce an opera written by an economist—would he? The communications director in me was relieved.

"But why did you have to support Lani Alvarez for mayor?"

He shrugged. "I find her entertaining."

"Doesn't it bother you that she sued the university and we had to waste a lot of our insurance company's money buying her off?"

"Not really. I'm tenured."

"Well," I told Mac before I left him at his office, "that was a fast trip to nowhere."

He looked pensive. "It would seem so, old boy. And yet I cannot shake the feeling that I have heard something significant this afternoon."

Chapter Twenty-Four
Copy Cat

"Optics?" Lesley Saylor-Mackie repeated.

I thought everybody knew that buzz word by now. Or maybe she just didn't understand how it applied in this case. Either way, I enlightened her. I always give her my best advice with no extra sugar, and she takes it or leaves it.

"It would look bad for SBU to make a play for the Bijou building from the widow Lattimore"—or was she the widow Davenport?—"so soon after the murder, in my professional opinion. Kendric sounded like he wanted to go public with our interest right away, as a strategy. I don't think that would sit well with the public, especially since word has gotten around town that we had a bit of a disagreement with Davenport over his proposed contribution of fifty big ones."

Or maybe you'd call it a confrontation. And it had happened a little more than a month earlier, right there in the Provost's office where we were having this discussion.

"Wasn't Davenport a generally unpopular figure?"

"As a person, yes. But some folks thought his planned hotel was a dandy idea, including half of City Council."

"I see. Kendric won't like this, but it's not a hard sell to get me to take the long view. That's my instinct as a historian. What do you think the chances are of that Ms. Thomas pulling together financing for an events center?"

I shrugged. "Beats me. Serena Mason turned down a chance to go into business with her, and Serena has the deepest pockets in town. But Gamble Bank is a possibility. Ms. Quong, or whoever approves loans with that many zeros, was willing to front Davenport the money to build a hotel at the site."

"Davenport had a track record as a top executive."

"But not as a developer. And it wasn't his idea to leave the executive suite at Amalgamated Brands, so his work record didn't impress me. Anyway, I think Brenda Thomas might have a shot at funding, but that's not going to happen overnight. You have plenty of time to make nice to Nadine and get her to sell the building to the university— or maybe even donate it."

"We already have an appointment for lunch a week from Friday at Ricoletti's Ristorante. We don't need to go public before then. Kendric's work on estimating the cost of restoring the Bijou building for our needs and finding the funding should occupy him well beyond that date."

I gaped. "Then you're two steps ahead of me on this. Why did you let me keep nattering on?"

"Because I wanted to hear what you had to say. You didn't disappoint me. What did you think of Maggie Barton's story this morning?"

It had appeared on the bottom of the local news page, under the headline **WOMEN PROFS PAID LESS AT SBU.** Ralph's head would have exploded.

"Could have been worse," I judged. "It wasn't on page one and it wasn't inaccurate. Your comments were to the point and helpful." The Provost had talked about her own positive experience as a woman on the St. Benignus faculty her entire academic career, but also vowed to find out if there were "institutional obstacles" that kept more women from achieving tenure and professorial rank.

"I do have some experience dealing with the press," the former mayor reminded me drily. "How is the murder investigation going?"

"Let's put it this way: It's a good thing Oscar's already lost most of his hair."

"Gibbons has a theory," Oscar said, handing Mac a cup of caffeinated coffee. It was lunch time and we were sharing sandwiches at the Chief's desk.

"That is unprecedented, is it not?"

"Close enough for horseshoes."

The assistant chief of Erin's small police force is a great cop. But he goes by the book, not trying to write his own, and doesn't talk unless he has something to say.

"I think maybe he's working this case a little harder than usual because the Schiff murder took place while he was hamming it up on stage as a super-whatever—an extra—just a few yards away. Right now, he's taking a run by Webster's house in the cruiser to make sure everything's okay. Anyway, his brainstorm is that instead of one killer, maybe whoever snuffed Schiff was a copycat trying to confuse things by using the M.O. of the Davenport murder."

"Oh, well done!" Mac said. "That is positively Agathachristiean in its ingenuity!!"

"If confusion was the goal, it sure worked," I noted.

"I think the idea's a little far-fetched myself, but it's not completely crazy," Oscar said. "I mean, Silverstein's Sunday story in the *Observer* included a lot of details from the coroner that a copycat could have used, including a general description of the murder weapon. I wouldn't have given Ben that much info." The Chief is not a huge fan of the media, although he's fond of Lynda and Johanna.

"Well, that's just ducky," I said. "Two victims and two murderers would add up to a quadruple headache."

Mac put down his half-pound hamburger. "As a thought experiment, I suggest we make a chart listing the victims along with potential killers and motives for each. Perhaps a graphic will bring some clarity. May I use your computer, Oscar?"

"Be my guest. *Mi computer es su computer.*"

"Murdoch would use a chalk board," I pointed out.

"Who?"

"Never mind. It's a TV show."

"And a series of novels," Mac said. "Detective Murdoch of the Toronto Constabulary has the distinct disadvantage of working about three-quarters of a century before the first personal computers were sold."

Mac sat at the Chief's laptop and created a three-column table in a new Word document as he spoke. "Now, let us divide the motives into 'personal' and 'functional.'"

"Isn't murder always kind of personal?"

"By no means, Oscar. Sometimes a murder victim is just a person standing in the way, as in the case of a customer shot during a bank robbery, for example. Mr. Davenport's wife and daughter might have personal reasons to kill him, for example, whereas for Brenda Thomas and Sheila Paxton homicide would be only a business tactic."

"Davenport's daughter is a nun," I reminded him. "Not only that, a cloistered nun. They don't get out. And why would she even want to kill him?"

"Perhaps he abused her in some way when she was a child. Come, Jefferson, this is a thought experiment! We are exploring possibilities, not probabilities."

Mac began to type. After about ten minutes, he had produced a simple chart:

VICTIM	PERSONAL MOTIVE	FUNCTIONAL MOTIVE
Hunter Davenport	*Nadine Lattimore* *Sr. Julia Davenport*	*Brenda Thomas* *Manny Templeton* *M.T.'s Source* *Sheila Paxton* *Kendric Armstrong*
Aaron Schiff	*Sally Henderson* *Vengeful student*	*Davenport's killer*

"Kendric has an alibi," I objected.

"In our experience, killers often do," Mac said mildly. He had me there. "The individuals I have listed in that column benefited either certainly or potentially from the demise of Hunter Davenport's plan to demolish the Bijou."

"Then you should have listed yourself," Oscar quipped before I had a chance at it. But you can't stop a train, so Mac rolled on:

"A possible exception is the shadowy figure I have listed as 'M.T.'s Source.' By that I mean whoever provided the information to Manny Templeton about the violations of the sunshine law at City Hall. That person must have a vested interest, but we have no idea what it was. Most likely, however, the intention was to ruin Mr. Davenport's development plans, for that was the major subject of the illegal talks. Perhaps the unknown whistleblower, disappointed that his or her revelations did not immediately derail the Front Street project, decided to take more drastic measures."

"What about the Henderson gal?" Oscar asked. "How does she make the list?"

"She seemed bereft at her betrothed's death, I grant you. However, it would be unwise not to include her. Passions by their very nature are unstable, and she certainly seemed passionate in our interview."

"She at least exists," I said. "That 'vengeful student' on your chart is pure fiction."

"I prefer to think of it as speculation, Jefferson. Surely as a teacher Aaron Schiff made enemies, though perhaps I should have added 'or parent,' given the spirit of our times."

"I guess by 'Davenport's killer' you mean that Schiff might have known something," Oscar said. "Or the killer thought he did." *The Man Who Knew Too Much!*

"Precisely."

"So that's everybody?"

"Not quite, Oscar. We have been considering potential murderers of Aaron Schiff because he is, after all, the one who was murdered. However, Jordan Webster, with good reason, appears to be convinced that *he* was the intended victim. Hence, Colonel Gibbons's observation of his home. So, let us augment our chart with one more row."

Mac returned to the computer to add:

Jordan Webster	*Temperamental singer*	*Lani Alvarez*
		Rival impresario
		Stanislaw Kroskof
		Someone who wanted to
		hurt the Erin Opera

"Lani Alvarez works for me," I said. "She's a loose cannon who might fire in any direction, as witnessed by her stupid picketing stunt. And sparks really flew between her and Webster at that publicity stunt of a news conference.

"But the other entries here aren't too helpful. Take the 'temperamental singer,' for instance. On the one hand, aren't all singers temperamental, especially opera singers?" *Everybody knows that.* "On the other hand, we haven't even gotten a whiff of any singer in this production with knives out for Webster." *So to speak.* "This is as theoretical as your vengeful student."

"Granted. However, I believe it is a theory worth considering. For that reason, I have invited the four principal singers in *Claudette* to our home for dinner tonight." The quartet he referred to was made up of Sarah Vanderhorst as Monique, Max Rohlfeld as Pierre Remaux, Scott Nash as Jean-Christophe de Lubac, and McCabe house guest Tiffany Carmichael in the title role. "I hope you and Lynda can join us as well, Jefferson."

"I think we're open. You didn't invite the other solo singers?" Monique's maid, Marie, and Claudette's undeclared lover, the hapless Jean Le Blanc, sang a few lines each.

"I spoke to Jordan Webster about them this morning. As it happens, they are a couple and both conservatory students that he barely knows. They were recommended by a friend. Their roles are so small that Mr. Webster allowed them to come to Erin for rehearsals only on the weekend so as to not disrupt their studies. It is scarcely credible that they would know anything, much less that they would be viable suspects."

"What about this 'rival impresario'? You don't seriously believe that the director of the Maysville Opera, if there is such a thing, would take a knife to his competitor?"

By this time Mac's "thought experiment" was starting to get on my nerves a little.

"Not seriously, no. Jordan Webster suggested that line of thought and I was trying to be comprehensive. If I have succeeded, then the killer's name appears somewhere on this chart."

As it turned out, it did.

"You really think the conductor, Kroskof, is chart-worthy?" I asked.

"Surely you observed the tension between him and Jordan Webster on Sunday?"

"But he's eighty-five if he's a day. He looks like he's going to topple over any minute! How could he stick a knife in anybody?"

"The maestro is eighty-two according to his biography on Wikipedia," Mac said. "And surely you know that an adrenaline rush has allowed individuals to accomplish feats of extraordinary strength."

"This is all very entertaining," Oscar interrupted, "but you can forget Kroskof. I heard him cutting Webster a new one, same as you did, so I had my men check to see if he was seen backstage between acts. I figured that with his tails he would stand out. It turns that under his contract he has a dressing room and hot tea delivered there during the intermission. He was seen there, and he wasn't seen anywhere else during the critical period."

"Very well." Mac highlighted the conductor's name and deleted it.

"Remind me to develop an eccentricity," I said. "It may come in handy someday."

Oscar snorted. "You already have more than your share. That catch-all last line—'Someone who wanted to hurt the Erin Opera'—shouldn't that apply to Hunter and Schiff, too?"

Mac looked chagrined. "Indeed it—"

Oscar's cell phone rang. He picked it up and looked at the name. "It's Gibbons," he announced. Then, into the phone, he said, "Hummel speaking. What? Hell's bells! Bring him in."

He hung up.

"You won't believe this. It's too damned easy. Gibbons caught a lurker hanging around the back of Webster's house, apparently trying to get in. And he has a knife."

Chapter Twenty-Five
Caught in the Act

Within the half-hour, I was trying to figure out why the guy on the hot seat in Oscar's office looked so familiar. He was probably in his mid-twenties, with a high forehead, strawberry-blonde hair worn long and curly at the back, and a wispy attempt at a short beard and mustache. He sat in a sullen slump, his hands in handcuffs. His wallet contained no identification, according to Gibbons, but he was nicely dressed in a Land's End windbreaker and chinos.

"What's your name?" Oscar demanded.

"John Smith."

"Not very original." *I'll say!* I immediately, and pointlessly, thought of Reginald Fortesque III calling himself "Scrappy Smith" when he first came to Erin.

"Is being unoriginal illegal?" Despite the snarky comeback, the man in the chair licked his lips nervously.

"No, but breaking and entering is."

William Shakespeare! That's who Oscar's guest had reminded me of. He looked like a younger version of portraits I'd seen of William Shakespeare—much younger, given that the Bard had been deceased more than 400 years.

He looked wild-eyed. "There was no breaking and entering!"

"Only because Colonel Gibbons didn't wait for you to make an entrance. He didn't want to put your intended victim's life in danger." This was nonsense, by the way. The guy hadn't had so much as a lockpick or a crowbar on him.

I figured Oscar was just playing with his catch, maybe trying to get a read on his nerve. "For now, trespassing will do as a charge to hold you on. But I expect we'll ramp it up in short order. I don't suppose you'd care to explain what you were doing skulking around with this knife."

He held it up, a wicked looking piece of metal. Or so it seemed to me.

Smith/Shakespeare barely glanced at it. "Am I in custody?"

"I think that's safe to assume."

"Then you have to read me my rights."

"Right you are, Mr. Smith. You have the right to remain silent and to not answer questions. Do you understand?"

He nodded, remaining silent.

As Mac and I looked on, also silent, Oscar proceeded through the rest of the Miranda warning liturgy. When he got to, "You have the right to speak to an attorney, and to have an attorney present during any questioning," Smith burst out with:

"I want Erica Slade."

Mac raised both eyebrows. "Interesting."

No doubt he was thinking what I was thinking, and Oscar said it: "Probably a good move for you. Since Ms. Slade doesn't normally stoop to handling trespassing cases, you must be looking ahead."

Our friend Erica, the best-known defense attorney in town, was hell on heels in the court room. Her clients didn't always walk, but they got a good shot at it. I wished I could have listened in on Smith's call to her.

This new wrinkle in the drama provided a lot of conversation material for the opera singers over dinner at Mac's house that night.

"So, this Smith actually had the knife on him?" said Sarah Vanderhorst, a tall, big-boned mezzo-soprano with long dark hair.

"He had *a* knife," Mac clarified. "I presume that examination of the blade could determine whether it had been tainted with the blood of the two dead men, although forensic analysis is not my métier."

"So, he was practically caught in the act," said Mac's house guest, Tiffany Carmichael. The soprano shivered and grabbed another piece of pizza. My sister being no dab hand at cooking, Mac had grilled several varieties of the always-popular comfort food on his patio. Mine had pineapple, green olives, and banana peppers.

"But you said Jordan wasn't even home at the time," observed Max Rohlfeld, a barrel-chested tenor with an image of "Betty Boop" tattooed on his arm and a dark beard on his face.

"He was probably going to lie in wait for him," I speculated.

"Perhaps," Mac said, as if making a concession. Well, wouldn't you also be a little miffed if a killer got caught in the act before you had a chance to display your sleuthing genius?

Lynda, equally chagrined at what appeared to be a fatal blow to her hopes of producing a hit podcast series out of the murders, was AWOL that night. She was seeing some chick flick with Triple M. Lynda's double pregnancy was not conducive to their other favorite outing together, martial arts lessons.

"Any idea why he did it?" asked bass-baritone Scott Nash. The opera's swarthy villain was the oldest of the four primary cast members, pushing forty. Tall and wide, he looked like a fellow who enjoyed a good party.

"We don't even know who he really is," I offered.

"Whoever and whyever, it's kind of disappointing," Ms. Carmichael said. "I was hoping for a more dramatic solution."

Opera singers!

Mac regarded her. "I gather from our previous conversation that you would prefer Grayson Caldwell to be the one with blood on his hands."

"Can we not talk about Caldwell's hands?" Nash said with a theatrical shudder.

Rohlfeld sniggered.

"You guys, too?" Sarah Vanderhorst asked. "I thought I was the only one in this opera he tried to paw."

"I was last year," Nash said. "That shouldn't count, except that he tried again last week. I finally had to make myself clear by getting physical with him, and not in the way he wanted."

"He offered me drugs," Rohlfeld put in. "Bad call on his part. I don't even like to take aspirin. I have a very delicate stomach." The news flash that Caldwell had been trying to trade pills for sexual favors lowered him further in my estimation, which I wouldn't have thought possible.

"Wow, I feel left out—and lucky," Tiffany Carmichael said. If she kept eating pizza like that, her slender figure was going to go the way of VHS tapes.

"Somebody needs to report this jackass to his bosses at the *New York Review*," Kate insisted. "No respectable publication would put up with a critic exerting sexual pressure on an artist."

"Don't be so sure," Ms. Vanderhorst said acidly. "The production bigwigs in Hollywood cover up for the A-list stars all the time."

"And vice versa, from what I hear," Nash kicked in.

"But if nobody speaks up, he'll just keep doing it!" my sister said.

Mac's dinner guests suddenly became quiet and very interested in their pizza.

Several months later a wave of sexual harassment allegations, few of them denied and even fewer credibly refuted, washed over Hollywood, Washington, and the national news media. Caldwell was among the least of the fish caught in the net.

"Were it not for John Smith's arrival on the scene," Mac said, "one might have speculated that Mr. Caldwell had somehow made the acquaintance of one or both of the victims with unfortunate consequences for them."

"Caldwell probably wouldn't bother with people he couldn't hurt career-wise," Ms. Carmichael said. "How could he pressure them?"

"And how would he even know the victims?" Rohlfeld added.

"The possibilities are endless," Mac said. "He could have encountered either one of them in a restaurant here in Erin, for example. Also, Grayson Caldwell attended the debut performance of *Claudette*, where Aaron Schiff was working backstage."

"Caldwell never came backstage, did he?" Nash asked the others. "I'd have noticed."

They all agreed that he hadn't.

"I don't remember seeing that Schiff guy, either," Nash added. "His picture in the paper didn't look familiar to me."

"He did to me, a little, I think," Tiffany Carmichael said. "But I couldn't swear to it."

"We know that Hunter Davenport wasn't at opening night," I said. *He was too busy getting killed.* "Did any of you ever see him around the Lyceum?"

That produced another negative consensus.

"I knew who he was," Rohlfeld volunteered. "I saw the name 'Davenport Development' splashed all over the program and a few other places as the presenting sponsor, so I asked Jordan what the deal was. I gather that without Davenport's money there would be no opera this season."

"Not that we're drinking champagne in our dressing rooms as it is," Sarah Vanderhorst said. "I knew this was a shoestring operation, but I thought it would at least be new shoestrings. Jordan is a brilliant artistic director, but I don't think he's the greatest money manager in the world."

"He should hire somebody to do that," I suggested.

"Using what to pay the salary?"

"How fortunate," Mac said, "that Mr. Davenport's widow has made it clear she intends to continue supporting the opera financially, perhaps to someone's dismay."

"Do you think this Smith guy, whoever he really is, had a grudge against Jordan?" Nash asked, bringing the conversation full circle.

Mac shrugged. "I am not yet convinced that he had anything to do with either murder."

Lynda was waiting for me at home, looking like the cat that ate the canary. Well, actually, being pregnant with our twins, she looked more like a cat that ate the canary cage.

"I had to tell you this in person. Polly knows the suspect, John Smith!"

Even though I couldn't see myself from the outside, I'm sure I delivered the shocked expression my beloved expected.

"How?"

"First I should say that she saw him in Oscar's lockup this afternoon." Triple M volunteers as a jail chaplain while not working at her day job in campus ministry at St. Benignus with Fr. Juan. "And she recognized him from when he was a student just a couple of years ago at SBU. He belonged to the Newman Center."

"Who is he, then? What's his real name?"

"That's the best part. His name's John Smith!"

Chapter Twenty-Six
The Confession

"Mr. Smith is involved in a romantic relationship with Lani Alvarez," Mac informed me the next day.

Isn't everybody?

"How do you know that?"

"Facebook, old boy."

"You found him on Facebook? How the heck did you narrow down the right one from all the other John Smiths on Facebook? Even in Erin there must be a dozen."

"That is why I took a different route. It seemed likely to me that Mr. Smith had a connection to someone else involved in this case. We knew from Sister Polly that he was a student at the university during the same period as Lani Alvarez, so I checked out her Facebook page. *Voilà!* It says she is in a relationship with John Smith."

"I hope he survives it," I quipped. "But just as importantly, he's in another kind of relationship with Erica Slade. I don't know how she's going to defend a guy caught red-handed, but you know she won't just roll over."

In that, however, I was surprised.

"My client is prepared to fully cooperate," she announced a few hours later over the table in Oscar's conference room. The Chief had invited Mac and me to sit in on his interview with Smith. Erica Slade, who has been known to socialize with the Codys on occasion, sat at his side. Erin's top defense counsel is on the wrong side of forty-five, but could pass for a decade younger on her best days. And this was one of her best days. She looked more like a model in a magazine ad for Cleopatra VII perfume than a take-no-prisoners defense attorney, what with her clingy blue dress, long raven hair, and stiletto heels.

"You mean he's going to confess to the murders?" Oscar asked. "Or just one of them?"

"Murders?" Smith squeaked. He looked like he'd slept in his clothes, if at all.

"Don't be silly, Oscar," Erica said. "My client knows nothing about the murders."

"I see this is going to take a while," Oscar said. "Coffee?"

"Is it Fair Trade?" Smith asked.

That brought Oscar up short for a second. Probably no "person of interest" had ever asked him that question before. "As a matter of fact, it is. Sister Polly insisted."

"She's a good person."

I had more than a hunch that Triple M's conversation with Smith yesterday afternoon had inspired his cooperative mood today.

After about five minutes of fiddling with the Keurig machine, Oscar had everybody mugged up. Erica took an espresso.

"So, Mr. Smith, for what perfectly innocent reason did you happen to be sneaking around Jordan Webster's house with a knife in your hand?" Oscar asked.

"There's no need to be sarcastic, Chief," Erica chided. "My client acknowledges that he was on the property in question without permission and that his intentions were not noble. It was a mistake, and Mr. Smith wishes to make a clean breast of it and attempt to make amends."

"Does he also wish to speak for himself or are you going to keep answering my questions for him, Slade?" Oscar's coffee apparently had not yet gone to work for the day.

She regarded Smith. "He can answer. I just wanted to set the stage."

"Go ahead," Oscar urged the miscreant.

Smith sat up straighter, looking miserable. "Okay. I was looking for a way to get into Webster's house so I could plant the knife to make it look like he did the murders."

What? Mac was so surprised he almost dropped his **I SEE NO REASON TO ACT MY AGE** mug.

"What the hell for?" Oscar asked.

"Lani was mad at him because of the way he treated her at the news conference on Tuesday. She wanted to get even by getting him into big trouble."

This was third-grade stuff!

"My client participated in his girlfriend's ill-considered scheme of revenge," Erica said. "He regrets his poor choice. They had argued a few nights before and he was eager to get back in her good graces."

"Yeah, I'm really sorry," Smith said. "It was stupid. But Lani kind of bewitched me." *Takes all kinds.*

"Just to be clear," Oscar said, "you're talking about Lani Alvarez, candidate for mayor?"

He nodded. "Right. We were in some classes together in college, but I never really knew her. Then when she announced for mayor, I volunteered to work on the campaign." He gave a sheepish grin. "She seemed to like me." *Like a cat likes a plush toy.* "I became very involved with the campaign, and then I became very involved with her." *Please stop there.* He did stop for a few seconds, then added: "I don't think I'm going to be seeing her anymore." *Better late than never.*

"How did you plan to get into the house? You didn't have any burglar tools on you."

"This is Erin. We were hoping he left it unlocked."

"Even if he had, and you'd gone in, that's still B&E. You're lucky you didn't get that far."

"Breaking and entering as a political tool has been rather unfashionable since a historical event generally known as Watergate," Mac advised Smith.

"What I was doing at Webster's house had nothing to do with the campaign. I told you, it was about Lani getting even."

"And you just went along with her?" Oscar was so entranced he hadn't even fired up an e-cig.

"She can be very, uh, persuasive." I was just as happy he didn't elaborate.

"The whole idea of framing Jordan Webster is bat-shit crazy, mister," Oscar advised. "He had the least reason of anybody in the world to kill his presenting sponsor, not to mention he was on stage at the time of Davenport's murder."

"I guess we didn't think that far ahead. But at least it might have given him a bad afternoon."

"You didn't think, period." Oscar would have made a good father.

"What did you do for the campaign, Smith?" I was curious.

"After a couple of weeks of campaigning door to door, I became her chief strategist." *That explains a lot.* "The news conference was my idea. We didn't have much money and we weren't getting any earned media. I thought we could get some publicity by piggy-backing on coverage of the murders. You have to admit it worked."

"Clearly, my client has a history of making poor judgements," Erica said. *No arguing with that.* "However, I can assure you that this misadventure has taught him a lesson. Putting him into the legal system at this point would not benefit society. On the contrary—"

"Not so fast," Oscar said. "Where did the knife come from, Smith?"

"I bought it at Walmart."

"Just for this stunt?"

"Right."

"So it's never been used?"

"No. I mean, no, it hasn't."

I could hear the wheels turning in Oscar's head, and so could Erica. "Forensic analysis will verify that," she said. "This knife didn't kill anybody."

"If that turns out to be the case, I see no reason to clutter up your ex-husband's caseload." Marvin Slade, Erica's former spouse and current bête noire (Mac's term) is Sussex County's prosecutor. Erica had become a defense attorney some years before just to spite him, giving the term "bitter divorce" new meaning. "I think we can let this slide unless Webster wants to prosecute for trespassing."

Erica smiled. "I've already spoken to Mr. Webster and he will be satisfied with a written apology."

Oscar summoned up his best scowl and trained it on John Smith. "Then get your ass out of here. And don't let me see you in trouble again." See what I mean? A great father.

Erica stood up, looking much taller than her five-seven because of the heels, and thrust out her hand. "Pleasure doing business with you, Chief."

"I bet."

Chapter Twenty-Seven
An Overlooked Suspect

"Shouldn't you at least go after Alvarez?" I asked when Erica had taken her lovely ankles and her client out of Oscar's domain.

"With what?" The Chief snorted and put another cartridge in his coffee machine. "I guess I could go to the prosecutor with a charge of conspiracy to frame Webster, but the poor doofus who was just in here would have to be a part of it. Do you really think I should do that to him?"

"Surely being enamored of Ms. Alvarez is penalty enough," Mac said.

"He may be cured of that," I noted.

"But he may not be, once he gets back in her clutches," Oscar said. He consumed caffeine. "And if he has second thoughts, and decides that stupid stunt was his own idea, then we've got nothing at all on her. Come to that, even with his testimony all we have is 'he said—she said.'"

"It also gets us no further in solving the murder," Mac pointed out.

"Nonsense." My voice oozed Cody-level sarcasm. "We've made great progress—all the way back to just where we were yesterday afternoon when Gibbons called."

"So," Oscar said with resignation, "it's back to the old drawing board."

"To our chart, to be more precise," Mac corrected him. "May I revisit your computer, Oscar?"

We gathered around the laptop. Oddly enough, Mac's chart hadn't changed since he'd inserted Jordan

Webster and removed Kroskof the day before. For my money, he should have made more cuts.

"You were going to add the line about somebody wanting to hurt the opera to the other two victims," Oscar pointed out.

Mac did so, so that he now had:

VICTIM	PERSONAL MOTIVE	FUNCTIONAL MOTIVE
Hunter Davenport	*Nadine Lattimore* *Sr. Julia Davenport*	*Brenda Thomas* *Manny Templeton* *M.T.'s Source* *Sheila Paxton* *Kendric Armstrong* *Someone who wanted to hurt the Erin Opera*
Aaron Schiff	*Sally Henderson* *Vengeful student*	*Davenport's killer* *Someone who wanted to hurt the Erin Opera*
Jordan Webster	*Vengeful singer*	*Lani Alvarez* *Rival impresario* *Someone who wanted to hurt the Erin Opera*

"What is there on this chart that we have missed?" Mac mused.

Oscar and I looked at each other.

"Lani Alvarez!" I said. "We didn't really talk about her before, and now we have more reason to. Maybe she wanted to frame Webster for the murder to take attention away from herself."

"And yet, old boy, she called attention to herself with that news conference."

"The old double bluff! Maybe you're thinking exactly the way she expected you to. The reason she gave Smith for the frame—according to him, anyway—was revenge for what Webster said at the news conference. You have to admit that's a pretty weak reason for anybody in her right mind to frame somebody for murder."

"'In her right mind' is the key," Oscar said. "Have you forgotten that we're talking about Lani Alvarez? Why did you put her on the chart to begin with, Mac?"

"So that we could have the satisfaction of eliminating at least one name." *Very cute.* "That was before I knew that Maestro Kroskof was untenable as a suspect."

"You may have put her under the wrong victim," I said. "Hunter Davenport was Bruce Gordon's biggest financial backer in the race for mayor. He was also a wealthy capitalist. Is it so far-fetched that Lani Alvarez stabbed him in a rage?"

"Actually, it's not," Oscar said. "In theory. I mean, I could see her doing that."

"Maybe it wasn't even premeditated."

"But what about Schiff?" the Chief asked. "Why kill him?"

"Once again, that oldie but goodie: The Man Who Knew Too Much. Suppose that he and Alvarez were friends and he provided her with the Pinkerton disguise—some old clothes of his and a fake beard swiped from the opera." I was on fire now.

"Your theory is marginally plausible," Mac judged, "except for the minor problem that Ms. Alvarez has an alibi."

I'd been waiting for this. "And how do we know that?"

"Because . . ." Mac stopped and got the funniest look on his face, like he'd just swallowed one of his huge Fuente Fuente Opus X cigars. "Because she said so."

"Exactly. *She said* during the news conference that she was picketing all during the opera. Does anybody else say so?"

"No." Oscar sat up. "We didn't ask. I'll have Gibbons go back to that parking lot attendant at the Lyceum—what was his name?"

"Scooter McBride," Mac supplied.

"Yeah, him. He was confident about when Nadine Lattimore went for her car. Let's see if he's that sure about Lani Alvarez."

"Why let Gibbons have all the fun?" I said. "Let's all go."

Mac drove me in his big red machine, while Oscar insisted that he and his deputy arrive in an official conveyance. I texted Lynda on the way to suggest that she might want to be in at the kill.

Scooter McBride had a day job as an attendant at the A-OK Parking Lot on Third Street. Cars were double-parked to squeeze in more vehicles, making it necessary for somebody like Scooter to move cars in and out. Since that part of town is dead at night, his services weren't needed there after business hours. Hence, he was available to pick up a few bucks when a performance was on at the Lyceum.

Mac and I pulled up about the same time Lynda arrived in her yellow Mustang. Scooter came out of his little hut and stared at both cars, although he'd parked the Chevy on the opening night of *Claudette*.

"I just love classic cars," he said.

"You remember my vehicle?" Mac said.

"Sure." He rattled off the license plate number without looking.

Scooter must have been about fifty, with hair more white than black. But his skin was unwrinkled by worry, and hustling between cars had kept him trim.

Oscar and Gibbons pulled up in the cop car.

"What's up?" Scooter sounded curious, not concerned.

"Just a few more questions," Gibbons said, unsmiling as usual. Somehow, he always seems to me like he's wearing sunglasses, even though he never does.

"Do you mind if I record this?" Lynda held out the gizmo.

Now he looked concerned. "What for?"

"You might be on a podcast."

"Really? Cool! I'm fine with that. Is this about the murder again?"

"It is," Mac said.

Oscar shot him a dirty look. The civilians were supposed to keep quiet, which was not a McCabe specialty. "Go ahead, Jack," he said to Gibbons, "since you handled the first round."

"Do you remember a young lady carrying a sign in front of the Lyceum on the night of the murder?"

"She was there every day of that opera, including Sunday afternoon."

"So you remember her?"

"Yeah, sure. She was loud and not very polite. Some of the people argued with her and she trash-talked back. My grandmother would have washed her mouth out with soap for using language like that."

"Did you park a car for her?"

He shook his head.

"Speak up," Lynda said, pointing at her recorder.

"No, she didn't have a car," Scooter said, louder than necessary. "She just showed up about a half-hour before everybody else and walked away when it was over."

A had a sinking feeling in my gut. This was not going the way I had expected.

"Okay, she walked away when it was over," Gibbons repeated. "But did she leave before that and come back?"

"No."

"Are you sure? This is very important."

"Yeah, I'm sure. I watched her. It gave me something to do. Nothing else happened except Miss Lattimore leaving at nine-fifteen in her Lexus, license number NL CH11."

"Why was the young lady picketing when the audience was already inside?"

"She yelled at anybody who walked by. It was quite a show, really."

"What did she do when she had the sidewalk to herself? Did she still carry the sign even though there was nobody to see it?"

That must have been Gibbons's way of testing to make sure that Scooter had been watching the whole time. The attendant didn't hesitate.

"Oh, she wasn't alone."

"What do you mean?"

"A few minutes after everybody else had gone in a guy came and started walking and talking with her. He was about her height with long, curly hair and what he probably thinks is a beard."

John "Shakespeare" Smith!

"He parked here," Scooter added. "The car was a 2014 model green Prius, license number DJ 2437 SX."

"When did he leave?"

"Maybe five minutes before everybody else came out and I got real busy."

So much for the idea that Smith had been playing mumbley-peg with Hunter Davenport while his girlfriend was establishing an alibi.

"You said the woman walked away," Gibbons said. "Didn't she drive away with the man?"

He shook his head. "They had an argument and he stalked off a few minutes before the opera was over."

"Did you hear what it was about?"

Scooter looked coy. "I wasn't eavesdropping."

"Of course not," Lynda said in an encouraging tone. "But you heard something anyway, didn't you?"

"It was hard not to. She had good lungs. She screamed something about he was a capitalist at heart and he yelled something about maybe so, but he didn't live off an allowance from his grandfather. Then she unloosed a bunch of four-letter words and he scrammed."

Gibbons looked around, as if to ask whether we had any more questions. We didn't.

"Thanks, Mr. McBride," Lynda said as she turned off her recorder.

"Sure thing. Hey, can I drive your Mustang around the block?"

Chapter Twenty-Eight
Whistleblower

"Aren't you glad you came?" Oscar asked me acidly.

"Okay, it was a dumb idea," I said.

"On the contrary, Jefferson," Mac boomed. "It was a brilliant idea! Regrettably, it was also a wrong one."

"And now we're dead in the water," Oscar said.

"Not so," Mac countered.

"But Alvarez was the only name on your silly chart that we haven't already looked at six ways from Sunday!"

"Not quite, Oscar. There is one more—not a name, to be precise, but a description. I refer to 'M.T.'s source,' whoever told Manny Templeton about the illegal meetings-by-text among City Council members."

"But we don't know who that is," I objected. "Only Templeton and his source know—or maybe Templeton's mother."

"Yes, his mother, Brenda Thomas. I believe that she is the key. I beg you to indulge us one more time, Oscar."

"I just know I'm going to regret this."

"Why did you ask me to come here?" Templeton demanded.

Because we thought you would be intimidated by the official surroundings of Oscar's office.

"Don't get so excited," Oscar said. "We just want to ask you a few questions."

"Don't you have to tell me I have the right to an attorney and all that crap?"

Oscar shook his head, which looked very official with his chief hat on. "That crap doesn't apply because you aren't in custody. Yet. At this point you can still leave here at any time."

Templeton got up.

"However, we thought perhaps you would like to defend your mother," Mac said mildly.

"What about my mother?" Something like panic lit up Templeton's eyes. He sat back down.

"Look at the facts, just like we did," Oscar said. "Your mother could be one of the big beneficiaries of Hunter Davenport's murder if she gets her act together to put an events center in the Bijou building. She's already got a track record in the wedding business, so she could make a bundle in this related venture. That's a serious motive."

"Don't be ridiculous."

"It doesn't sound so far-fetched to me," I said, right on cue.

"I'm not even sure Mom has what it takes to run that kind of business. It's a whole different thing from ordering flowers and hiring musicians. And who would kill somebody just for the chance to *maybe* buy an old building?"

"Lots of people," Oscar assured him. "Want some java?"

"No, I want to leave."

But he didn't move while Oscar helped himself to the Keurig machine. "So, here's the thing, Manny. Yeah, murder is a pretty drastic step. But that wasn't the first step. Your mom first tried to bring down Davenport by getting you to spread the news that Council members were violating the state open meetings law. You aren't the civic gadfly with a noble purpose that you made yourself out to be. You were trying to block the Bijou demolition to help your mother."

"She wouldn't kill anybody!"

"Are you so certain? She did somehow learn of the City Council skullduggery and ask you to take it to the media, did she not?" Mac spoke unthreateningly, good-cop style. He didn't know whether what he said was true or not. That's why he'd called this ploy a "charade."

"No, it wasn't her. Mom didn't even know about it until after I'd done it."

"You can't expect us to believe that," Oscar said. *Bad cop.*

"It's the truth."

"If not your mother, then who?" *Good cop.*

"Allison Channing."

"At City Hall?" I said, stunned. But no more stunned than Templeton, judging by the look on his face. Apparently, the name had popped out of his mouth without permission from his brain. "The administrative assistant?"

"Yeah, that's her," he mumbled. "The dragon at the gate."

"I was wondering when you were going to figure it out," Allison said. "I thought for sure it was a tip-off when I arranged for Johanna's Freedom of Information filing to be answered so quickly. When has that ever happen before?"

Mac winced. "I stand before you humbled and embarrassed that I did not deduce you as Manny Templeton's source. Who would know better than you what our esteemed Council members were up to, other than they themselves?"

She snorted. "Those guys come and go, and most of 'em can't go too soon to suit me."

It was late in the day and we had the big anteroom at City Hall all to ourselves, although I doubted the veteran bureaucrat would have been any more circumspect if the place had been full. Allison Channing, looking proud of herself, was in a bean-spilling mood.

"Even now I do not understand," Mac confessed. That made three of us. Oscar's broad face was one big question mark. "What was your motivation? And why use Manny Templeton as your tool?"

"I wouldn't call him that. He knew what he was doing. His mom, Brenda, is a friend of mine. We go running together. I'm old and she smokes, so it works out. She told me about this idea she had for the Bijou and how it was all going to hell in a handbasket because this hot-shot developer bought the property and was going to build a hotel there.

"When I figured out from words dropped here and there what Gordon and his minions were doing in secret, that really peeved me. I figured there was probably text evidence, dumb as they are. But I was too much of a coward to go public myself, which is what I should have done. And I didn't want Brenda to drop the bomb, because her self-interest was obvious. I thought of Manny. He really is civic-minded, and his connection to Brenda isn't obvious because they have different last names. Manny went for it before I even finished telling him what I had in mind. Just between you three and me, he kind of likes the limelight."

No secret there.

Mac and Oscar looked like they were thinking hard about all this. I just had a headache.

"Your little scheme created a big brouhaha and a lot of embarrassment for our beloved city fathers and mothers," Oscar said at last. "But it didn't stop the Zoning Board of Appeals from okaying the demo of the Bijou. So, you had to kill Hunter Davenport."

Allison's laugh wasn't forced. "What have you been smoking, Chief? Brenda Thomas is a good gal, but I don't like her *that* much. Just the sight of blood makes me feel faint. Do you have any more questions?"

"I think not," Mac said, his tone subdued. His long-held notion that the Templeton's tipster was a key player in this drama had gone the way of his afternoon office cigar.

"Then I have a question for you, Professor McCabe." She pointed to the "Night at the Music Hall" poster in her cubicle, the one with the stylized illustration of "McCabe the Marvelous, Master of All Mysteries." "What's your big trick going to be?"

Mac must have felt like he owed her an answer, because he didn't temporize.

"Given the Music Hall theme, I could not resist performing my own version of a classic effect: I will make Kate disappear before your very eyes, and then reappear in a box that has been suspended over the stage in full view of the audience during the entire act."

Apparently, that's easier than solving two murders.

Like his amateur sleuth, Mac had once been a professional stage magician, spending some time at it in Europe during a misspent (or well-spent) youth after graduating from what was then St. Benignus College.

"How in the world—?"

"A magician, like a gentleman, never tells. Suffice it to say that the act is an illusion, Miss Channing, and the operating principle of most illusions is the same: Whereas a sleuth not only sees, but observes, an illusionist makes his audience see that which is not—"

He stopped dead.

"Which is not what?"

"Eh? Oh. Which is not actually there, of course. Because one sees what one expects to see—believing is seeing, as it were. And I have just realized, at long last, that is what the murderer of Hunter Davenport and Aaron Schiff counted on!"

"You mean you know who the killer is?" Oscar demanded.

"I believe so. And you are going to get the proof."

ACT THREE

Chapter Twenty-Nine
Behind the Mask

"But we've ruled out every name on your blessed chart," I objected to Mac as we left City Hall. Or maybe I didn't say "blessed."

"Not quite, old boy."

And he explained.

"Well, I'll be damned," Oscar said. "And that proof you mentioned?"

"I believe I know where you can find the weapon. You will need a search warrant."

"If we find it, that's good enough for me. I'll bring the killer in."

"May I suggest there is a better way?" Mac said. "There is another person who deserves to see us confront the guilty party."

The next evening found Mac, Oscar and me at Nadine Lattimore's spacious home, a horizontal design strongly influenced by the Prairie School of architecture. Lynda had begged to go along, digital recorder in hand, but Oscar had growled that he wasn't going to let this become any more of a circus than it already was.

But he didn't tell me not to bring a recorder.

We sat in the massive living room, Nadine sharing a maroon leather couch (or was it a love seat?) with Jordan Webster. She looked more rested than I'd seen her since the murder, and even her long chestnut hair seemed to have more bounce and gloss. Webster, decked out in a red turtleneck that clashed with the color of the couch, looked like he'd been biting his nails.

A "For Sale" sign had been posted by Happy Homes Realty outside the house.

"I'm not leaving Erin," Nadine assured us. "I just can't live in this house knowing that Hunter died here."

That made her a motivated seller, which meant that somebody was going to get a good deal. Lynda and I had saved thousands of dollars on our house because of the body in the freezer.[7]

"That is quite understandable," Mac rumbled. "It is, of course, about your husband that we are here to speak with you."

"You mean about his murder, and who did it?"

"Quite so. I would appreciate your patience as I explain. This will take a while." He paused, maybe mentally reviewing his script. Although he'd already spilled it all to Oscar and me, he had a very different audience now.

"My moment of clarity came all too late, when I finally realized that we had all been prey to a very simple illusion. I will get back to that in due course. Kate should have pointed me toward the truth with her observation immediately after the second murder. She said that killing Mr. Davenport and then Mr. Webster here, which seemed to be the intention, was a ridiculously round-about way of sabotaging the Erin Opera. Indeed, it would have been. If that were the real goal, it could have been accomplished by one murder—that of Mr. Webster. And, in fact, the opera was not hurt at all by the murderer's actions. Mr. Webster was not killed, and the important financial support formerly provided by Hunter Davenport will continue to be supplied by his widow."

"It's not the killer's fault that I'm still here," Webster piped up. "I just got lucky. And he had no way of

---

[7] See "A Cold Case" in *Rogues Gallery* (MX Publishing, 2014).

foreseeing that Nadine would step up to be the season sponsor. Nobody knew that would happen."

Mac turned to Nadine. "Surely anyone familiar with the situation would have known that you were the opera aficionado in your family."

"I suppose so."

"I don't know what you're getting at," Webster huffed, "but Hunter was very important to the opera."

"His money was, at any rate," Mac said. "I do not dispute that. In fact, it was so crucial that you went against all your instincts as an artist and supporter of the arts and refused to sign our 'Save the Bijou' advertisement. To your credit, you were not coy about your reasons. You said you did not want to offend your season sponsor by opposing his pet project. Do you remember?"

Webster glanced at me, maybe realizing that I was a witness. "I remember."

"That was very understandable, given that Hunter Davenport had a reputation for playing rough. He would not likely have taken kindly to your opposition, nor would he have let it go unpunished. And yet a few weeks later, on the day of the Conservation Board hearing, you asked me for a yard sign."

"My conscience bothered me. I had to do the right thing, no matter the consequences."

Mac arched an eyebrow. "Oh? You gave a different reason at the time. You claimed then to be persuaded by comments from Ms. Larkin and Mr. Pennington. And yet I am inclined to believe that you had a more concrete reason, just as Bruce Gordon had a reason for his change in the opposite direction. Mr. Gordon had something to gain— money in the form of campaign contributions from a man who wanted his support in the mayor's office. I believe that you no longer had something to lose—season sponsorship from the same man. Hunter Davenport had recently informed you that that he would not be supplying his crucial support of the opera next year."

"How do you know that?" Nadine asked.

"In candor, I cannot claim to know it beyond all doubt. There are, however, strong indications that was the case. The season sponsorship was fifty thousand dollars. Your husband offered the same amount to St. Benignus University in a thinly veiled attempt to buy my withdrawal from the field. When that failed, he invested—and I use that term with malice aforethought—almost exactly the same amount of money in Bruce Gordon's mayoral campaign. All his contributions through the various LLCs added up to forty-nine thousand, five hundred dollars. It could scarcely be a coincidence that the same number keeps coming up. I believe it means that Hunter Davenport found a more productive place to put fifty thousand dollars."

"Hunter complained in the last few weeks before his murder about the financial mess at the Erin Opera, the cost overruns," Nadine said, almost as if to herself. "Maybe he was working his way up to telling me that he was going to pull out."

"Successful business people are not in the habit of giving money to unsuccessful enterprises, not even to non-profits as an act of charity," Mac pointed out.

"That's bullshit," Webster declared.

"I do not believe so. Brenda Thomas told us that you solicited Serena Mason for financial support. I have confirmed with Serena that you asked her to be the presenting sponsor three weeks ago, which would have been just after that May 3 hearing at which you asked for a 'Save the Bijou' yard sign. That can only mean that Mr. Davenport had told you shortly before of his intent to cease that role. When did that happen? Most likely it was during a meeting with you on April 28."

"We didn't pay much attention to the appointment with you when we looked at the calendar in Davenport's smartphone," Oscar told Webster, almost apologetically. "We kind of focused on Gordon and ignored your name because it seemed natural that he would be meeting with you. You had an established relationship."

Mac continued:

"When the notably generous Serena Mason turned down your request for season sponsorship, Mr. Webster, you must have been desperate. Perhaps you even thought of approaching your true champion, Ms. Lattimore here. You must have known, however, that a news anchor in the thirty-sixth largest media market in the country, although by most standards well compensated, was scarcely positioned to make an annual donation of fifty thousand dollars to the Erin Opera Company. If only she had her husband's wealth . . . And this must have been when you realized that, contrary to outward appearances, the opera would *benefit* by Hunter Davenport's death, not be hurt by it."

By some strange magic of body language, Nadine seemed to move away from Webster without actually doing so. "You're saying . . ." She couldn't finish the sentence, so she started a new one. "That's just surreal."

"You find the future of the opera company an insufficient motive for murder?" Mac asked her rhetorically. "Remember, Ms. Lattimore, what you yourself observed on the afternoon of Aaron Schiff's murder: Jordan Webster not only founded the Erin Opera, he wrapped up his entire identity in the enterprise and therefore in its success. He had failed as a singer, but he would not fail as an impresario. He controlled everything about the company, even to the point of changing the original name Luther Kressel had given to his opera.

"Unfortunately, whatever his artistic skills, Mr. Webster was totally lacking in the necessary business acumen to manage even a small opera."

"I resent that," Webster snapped.

"Resent it all you want," Oscar volleyed back. "It's the truth. Thanks to the online service GuideStar, we read the Form 990 you filed with the IRS for last year. It wasn't pretty. I'm sure Davenport saw the same financials."

"And those numbers supported the picture that emerged from our discussion with the Erin Opera singers—that of a management in financial chaos," Mac added. "You needed money badly to save your dream and therefore your self-esteem. And you killed Hunter Davenport to get it."

"But Hunter was killed during the second act of *Claudette*," Nadine protested, grasping the only straw that was left to her. "Jordan was on stage at the time."

"That is what you saw because that is what you expected to see, the wellspring of many illusions," Mac said. "The great Houdini disappeared in full view of the audience by the simple process of rapidly changing his clothing and blending in with a group of others similarly dressed on a crowded stage. Your assumption that Mr. Webster was the supernumerary in the Baron Samedi mask was reinforced by a front-page photo in the *Observer* making that identification in the caption. That caption was so helpful to Mr. Webster that he carried it with him and described it for the listeners of Lynda's podcast-in-progress.

"In truth, however, Aaron Schiff was beneath that mask on the opening night, just as he was three days later. That is why he had to die: Only he knew that Jordan Webster had no valid alibi for the time of your husband's death. Sooner or later, Mr. Schiff would have suspected that the artistic director had driven to this home and stabbed his patron. Having visited here many times, Mr. Webster, you were aware of the video security system and the need to don a disguise—one readily available from stage costumes and makeup.

"You intended all along, did you not, that Aaron Schiff would appear to have been killed by mistake instead of you? The notion of an attempt on your life fit in very nicely with the falsehood—we might even call it another illusion—that the death of Hunter Davenport was a blow to the Erin Opera."

The killer's name had been on Mac's chart, just as he'd said—but as an intended victim, not a suspect. I'll leave it up to you whether you think that's playing fair.

Webster sighed. "I think you've been reading your own books too much." *He's heard that before, from his wife.*

"What about proof?" Nadine asked.

"We have the murder weapon," Oscar said. He addressed Jordan. "You hid it at the Lyceum in a box of props from the opera, but it was no prop knife. Mac had the bright idea that it might be there, and Gibbons found it."

"After you spoke to Lynda for her podcast in the wake of Aaron Schiff's murder, you tried to stop me when I bent down in the direction of the prop boxes," Mac reminded Webster. "You relaxed, however, when I picked up the Baron Samedi mask from a costume box instead. Although that meant nothing to me at the time, it later seemed significant."

"Any fingerprints on that knife?" Webster asked in a way that made it clear he knew the answer.

"No, it was wiped clean," Oscar admitted, "which is suspicious right off the bat even if it weren't already obvious it's a real knife and not a stage phony like the others in the box. But blood doesn't come off that easily, and it can be typed. So, we can prove it's the knife that killed Davenport and Schiff, and it was in a box that was under your control.

"We've got something even better, though." Oscar was loving this. He held up a piece of paper. "This is a warrant to examine your cell phone. If you sent any text messages from here, or someplace between the Lyceum and here, when you were supposed to be on stage, the GPS in your phone will show where you were."

"But I didn't send any—" He stopped, realizing he had blown it.

"Oh, Jordan." Nadine's voice rang with despair and her beautiful green eyes began to fill up with tears.

As Webster moved his right hand, I suddenly remembered that he'd carried a gun in his right front jeans pocket. That was not a good thing to forget until now. Oscar and Mac (concealed carry) were both armed as well, but that would be cold comfort if a shoot-out erupted in Nadine's living room.

Webster's hand kept moving, however, and he pulled a handkerchief out of his back pocket. He wiped his face with it.

"You didn't read me my rights." Webster sounded petulant, like a little kid yelling "unfair!"

"Up to now you haven't been in custody, my friend," Oscar said. "That just changed. Jordan Webster, you are under arrest. You have the right to remain silent and to not answer . . ."

That never gets old for Oscar.

Chapter Thirty
Voice of the Dead

"Crap!" I exclaimed as we got into Mac's car.

"Something is amiss, Jefferson?"

I held up Lynda's digital recording gizmo, which I'd had in my pocket. "I thought I was recording everything for Lynda, but somehow I screwed up. She won't be happy."

"You have my sympathy." Mac's thumbs danced over his smartphone. "I am sending Kate a text, asking her to come over. I think that Ms. Lattimore will welcome the company."

"How did the county crime lab analyze the knife for blood so quickly?" I asked. "I thought they were drowning in drug cases."

"Let us say that Oscar overstated the case by implication. The knife is on its way to the BCI[8] laboratory as we speak. I am confident that they can confirm our deduction in a week or two."

Mac was right, but by that time Jordan Webster was dead and buried.

Erica Slade got him out on bail the day after Oscar arrested him. I don't know where the bail money came from and I haven't tried to find out. But I don't think it was Nadine Lattimore. Two days later, Webster was the coroner's latest drug overdose—this one on purpose. But before he went gentle into that good night, he sent a WAV

---

[8] The Ohio Bureau of Criminal Identification and Investigation has three crime labs which often perform tests for local jurisdictions.

file to Lynda at her Grier e-mail still listed on the *Observer* website. She listened to it, then forwarded it to Mac and me. We listened to it separately, and then together in my office, with Popcorn making an audience of three.

And this is what we heard:

Hello, Ms. Teal. This is Jordan Webster. I've decided not to stick around for a trial. Even if Ms. Slade managed to beat the rap for me, the Erin Opera Company and everything I've worked for is dead. I have no choice really, just like I had no choice when Hunter decided to pull the plug on his sponsorship.

Since you're going to produce a podcast about this business, I want it to be more than just another triumph of the obnoxious Sebastian McCabe. I want it to include my side of the story, and I'm the only one who can give it to you. So here goes.

The Erin Opera Company means everything to me. You've heard that from Nadine, and it's true. I was stunned when that arrogant jerk Hunter told me he was tired of pouring money down the drain that could be put to a better use. Instead of offering to help me on the business side where we had some problems, he just bailed. I tried to find a replacement sponsor, but it was no good.

I knew there was one person who would help me, though: Nadine. She loved opera and wanted it to thrive in her hometown. Just for the record, that was the only thing between us—her enthusiasm for what I was doing. I feel bad that I let her down and the Erin Opera Company won't survive. And for her sake I don't feel so good about killing her husband, either. But, like I said, I had no choice about that once it hit me that Nadine would help once she was free of him.

You have to admit it was pretty clever the way I tried to avoid getting caught. I made that appointment with Hunter under a fake name, promising some dirt on the leading opponent of his Bijou project. I knew he was the kind of guy who would fall for that. Then I stabbed him with a knife that had belonged to my father. I think he picked it up in Vietnam. I don't remember much about the stabbing, except that once I got started I kind of got carried away.

Meanwhile, Aaron Schiff was taking my part in the Mardi Gras scene. I asked him to do it as a favor because I didn't feel well. Everybody says he was a nice guy, and maybe he was, but he thought a little too much of himself to suit me. Nevertheless, I didn't originally plan to kill him. It only came to me later that was something else I had to do. He was probably too naïve to figure out the alibi thing, but he still might have mentioned to the cops in passing that he'd replaced me on the murder night. That might not mean a lot by itself, but it would seem suspicious that I hadn't told them.

So, I asked Aaron to take another turn as Baron Samedi in the final performance, figuring that when I stabbed him the same way I did Hunter it would look like somebody was trying to kill me. It worked for a few days, but not long enough. I guess it wasn't so clever after all.

I've never done hard drugs, but I know where to get them. It won't take much to put me away. I hope that doesn't mean the bail money is forfeited.

I'm sorry we won't get to do another season. I was looking forward to Madame Butterfly.

"Can you believe that he called me obnoxious?" Mac demanded.

Yes.

"This should get you out of hot water with Lynda, Boss," Popcorn said. "It's better than what you would have recorded at Nadine Lattimore's house if you hadn't flubbed it."

Thanks for bringing that up.

"If you ask me," I said, although no one did, "Jordan Webster was a couple of arias short of an opera, like most people who kill themselves. Why didn't he just use that gun he carried, the Beretta Pico?"

"Guns are seldom used in opera, old boy," Mac reminded me. "Stabbing and poison are much more common. The use of the blade in both murders should have been a clue that the killer was deeply involved in opera, as should the name Pinkerton."

"What do you mean?"

"Something about the pseudonym the killer chose for his meeting with Hunter Davenport nagged at me. And yet the significance eluded me even though Jordan Webster and Luther Kressel both mentioned *Madame Butterfly*, an opera in which the title character dispatches herself in the last act with a knife. Butterfly's perfidious lover was an American naval officer named Pinkerton. Jordan Webster probably chose the name without even thinking that it came from one of his favorite operas.

"In the end, it was his tragic flaw of hubris, his inability to accept his own limitations, or the failure of his dream that caused him to kill and ultimately brought about his own destruction. Quite operatic, really. One might call it Greek and Shakespearean, for that matter."

Somebody better keep an eye on Warren Burch, I thought. His departure as dean of the Gulliver Mackie School of Business and Economics, which he regarded as his personal fiefdom, was still being negotiated.

Mac's reference to Shakespeare reminded me of the bard's look-alike, John Smith.

"I guess it's a good thing Oscar decided not to fool with charges against Smith and Alvarez," I said. "After all, Webster was guilty of what they were trying to frame him for."

Chapter Thirty-One
And So It Goes

Will this mayoral campaign never end? And will it never stop changing? Reverend Sutterlee has jumped into the fray as a credible write-in candidate, hoping to strike "acting" off his temporary title. Ben Silverstein speculated in print just this morning that Reginald "Scrappy" Fortescue may pull out in his favor. John Smith, meanwhile, has left the Alvarez campaign—and Alvarez. Stay tuned.

Scrappy's complaint against Bruce Gordon with the Erin Elections Commission is still pending. Maybe it will get decided sometime before the next election in four years.

The ultimate destiny of the Bijou is still up for grabs. But after several lunches with Nadine Lattimore, Saylor-Mackie is hopeful she can get her to donate the building to SBU as a performance venue named after Hunter Davenport. It could also be used by the Erin Opera for large productions—such as *Aida*—that wouldn't fit well on the smaller Lyceum stage. My money is on the Provost to pull it off.

About the Erin Opera: It didn't die with Jordan Webster. Nadine was so determined to show that it could thrive without him that she convinced the opera board (a rather supine bunch, just as in the Webster days) to appoint her as artistic director. Rehearsals are underway for the new season, starting not with *Madame Butterfly* but with *The Magic Flute*.

Grayson Caldwell will not be reviewing it, by the way, at least not for the *New York Review*. Max Rohlfeld, perhaps encouraged by Kate's shaming, complained to the magazine about his sexual harassment. Predictably, that unleashed a flood of similar complaints. *NYR* was upfront about his dismissal, sending a clear "no-tolerance" message in a strongly worded statement. Caldwell, the weasel, has admitted nothing other than "consensual dalliances."

Nadine is also heavily involved, along with business partner Sheila Paxton, in lobbying the City Council to acquire that seven miles of former railroad track to expand the bike trail along the Ohio. The smart money says they will succeed. I doubt if Nadine will ever get back to her anchorwoman gig, but her "ratings" in the hearts of her fellow citizens have never been higher.

Lynda's six-part podcast, "Murder at the Opera," was an over-the-top success, with more than a million downloads in the first month. This could take her to new heights in her profession. Or maybe not. Journalism is a funny business these days, so Lynda is working like a demon in the evenings to finish her novel *Bluegrass*. She figures she won't have much time to fiddle with fiction when the twins get here. She's a wise woman, my wife.

A Few Words of Thanks

Readers of Jeff Cody's chronicles of Sebastian McCabe who have read the acknowledgements page—and I hope many have—must have long ago realized that the byline should be "Dan Andriacco and Team." The team varies a bit from adventure to adventure, but for the most part it's a case of "round up the usual suspects."

So, thanks again to:

Ann Brauer Andriacco, for her constant assistance and encouragement, as well as her readership;

Jeff Suess, for proofreading and final preparation of the manuscript; and

Steve Winter, yet again, for giving the manuscript the incredible benefit of his engineering eye.

And special thanks this time to my brother, Tony Andriacco, for providing most of the names in the story.

As always, this book never would have seen the light of day without the efforts of publisher Steve Emecz and cover illustrator Brian Belanger. I'm proud to be part of MX Publishing's social enterprise venture.

About the Author

Dan Andriacco has been reading mysteries since he discovered Sherlock Holmes at the age of nine, and writing them almost as long.

The first eight books in his popular Sebastian McCabe–Jeff Cody series are *No Police Like Holmes, Holmes Sweet Holmes, The* 1895 *Murder, The Disappearance of Mr. James Phillimore, Rogues Gallery* (shorter stories), *Bookmarked for Murder, Erin Go Bloody* and *Queen City Corpse.* He is also the co-author, with Kieran McMullen, of *The Amateur Executioner, The Poisoned Penman,* and *The Egyptian Curse* mysteries solved by Enoch Hale with Sherlock Holmes.

Also the author of *Baker Street Beat: An Eclectic Collection of Sherlockian Scribblings,* Dan is the leader of the Tankerville Club of Cincinnati; a member the Illustrious Clients of Indianapolis, the Agra Treasurers of Dayton, and the Vatican Cameos; and an associate member of the Diogenes Club of Washington, D.C.—all scion societies of the Baker Street Irregulars. Follow Dan's long-running blog at www.danandriacco.com, his tweets at *@DanAndriacco,* and his Facebook Fan Page, Dan Andriacco Mysteries.

Dr. Dan and his co-conspirator, Ann Brauer Andriacco, have three grown children and six grandchildren. They live in Cincinnati, Ohio, USA, about forty miles downriver from Erin.

Praise for the earlier Sebastian McCabe–Jeff Cody mysteries

"Dan Andriacco's *Queen City Corpse* is the latest in his series about Jeff Cody and Sebastian McCabe, who are in Cincinnati for a mystery convention and encounter mystery and murder, and a surprising solution; it's a lively story."
—Peter Blau in *Scuttlebutt from the Spermaceti Press*

"This (*Queen City Corpse*) is the seventh novel in a deliciously literate, witty series, with ingenious plots and engaging characters. Highly recommended!"
—*Sherlock Holmes Society of London*

"This (*Erin Go Bloody*) is Dan Andriacco's best book to date! I feel I could actually walk around downtown Erin, Ohio and not get lost. The characters are charming and believable. These are always entertaining reads! I have become a huge fan of Mac and Jeff!"
—Retired Sheriff Kenneth Ramsey, Sr.

"The ingenious twist at the end is an example of Andriacco's masterful ability to pen a page-turner. *Bookmarked for Murder* is a must-read for anyone who loves a classic who-done-it."
—Mystery writer Kathleen Kaska

"You're in the hands of a master of mystery plotting here. *Rogues Gallery* is a delightful read, hard to put down, and highly recommended. And did I say fun?"
—Screenwriter and novelist Bonnie MacBird

"The villain is hard to discern and the motives involved are even more obscure. All-in-all, this (*The Disappearance of Mr. James Phillimore*) is a fun read in a series that keeps getting better with each new tale."
—Philip K. Jones

"*The* 1895 *Murder* is the most smoothly-plotted and written Cody/McCabe mystery yet. Mr. Andriacco plays fair with the reader, but his clues are deftly hidden, much as Sebastian McCabe hides the secrets to his magic tricks under an entertaining run of palaver."
—*The Well-Read Sherlockian*

"I loved Dan Andriacco's first novel about Sebastian McCabe and Jeff Cody, and I'm delighted to recommend (*Holmes Sweet Holmes*), which has a curiously topical touch."
—Roger Johnson, *Sherlock Holmes Society of London*

"*No Police Like Holmes* is a chocolate bar of a novel—delicious, addictive, and leaves a craving for more."
—*Girl Meets Sherlock*

Also from MX Publishing

Visit www.mxpublishing.com for dozens of other Sherlock Holmes novels, novellas, short story collections, Conan Doyle biographies, Holmes travel books, and more.

MX Publishing is the award-winning, world's largest independent Sherlock Holmes Book publishers with over 60 new authors and 100 new Sherlock Holmes stories in print.

www.ingramcontent.com/pod-product-compliance
Lightning Source LLC
Chambersburg PA
CBHW071329250626
47159CB00004B/1524